The TREE Is OLDER Than YOU ARE

Burbujas de amor (*Bubbles of Love*), Carmen Esquivel

The TREE Is OLDER Than YOU ARE

A Bilingual Gathering
of Poems & Stories
from Mexico
with Paintings
by Mexican Artists

SELECTED BY

Naomi Shihab Nye

SIMON & SCHUSTER
BOOKS FOR YOUNG READERS

SIMON & SCHUSTER BOOKS FOR YOUNG READERS
An imprint of Simon & Schuster Children's Publishing Division
1230 Avenue of the Americas
New York, NY 10020
Copyright © 1995 by Naomi Shihab Nye
Pages 106-109 constitute an extension of the copyright page.
A special thanks to The Horse's Mouth for keyboarding and proofreading assistance.
All rights reserved including the right of reproduction in whole or in part in any form.
SIMON & SCHUSTER BOOKS FOR YOUNG READERS is a trademark of Simon & Schuster.
Designed by Christy Hale
The text of this book is set in Latin 725.
Manufactured in Mexico
10 9 8 7 6 5 4 3 2 1

Library of Congress Cataloging-in-Publication Data
The tree is older than you are ; a bilingual gathering of poems & stories from
Mexico with paintings by Mexican artists / selected by Naomi Shihab Nye.
p. cm.
1. Mexican literature. 2. Mexican literature—Translations into English.
3. Mexican poetry—20th century. 4. Mexican poetry—
20th century—Translations into English.
I. Nye, Naomi Shihab.
PQ7235.T74 1995
860.9'972—dc20   95-1565 CIP AC
ISBN 0-689-80297-8

*For everybody, but especially for
the young Mexican-American writers
who are the long branches and
who have seen the rivers
come out of their pencils
more than once*

Fotografía (Photography), Enrique Flores

INTRODUCTION

My first time in Mexico, I stood shivering on the beach at Tampico in the moonlight as hundreds of glossy sand crabs scuttled in and out of their holes. Their intricate zigzagging fascinated and terrified me. I was seven years old, guarding my feet. All night they would be stitching the sand together, on the beach and in my roaring dreams. They would stay with me forever in one word: mystery. The surf crashed noisily and high, gurgling with bits of tar which stuck to the skin while swimming.

We had driven into Mexico to locate some distant Palestinian relatives who had emigrated there before my father emigrated to the United States, and although we stayed for days visiting a warm and friendly family, I never felt completely convinced that they were the people we had been looking for. Presumably my father did. I was much more interested in the Mexico which held

them ("the blue which was really blue" I called it later): secret patios, high iron doors, vines spilling over walls.

What can people carry of a country that is not theirs? The slant of light, holding open its good strong hands. Holding everything without dropping it. The smiles of neighbors, waving from windows, saying come here, come in, *bienvenidos*, welcome!

We sat on a roof among the startling radiance of pinned white sheets, breathing the sweetness of laundry. Three languages bumped and tumbled. My brother and I peeled tiny fresh bananas on a high sunstruck balcony. Open streets filled with voices calling, calling. A new scent of the ancient life of the world.

Later, home in the gloomy gray winter of the midwestern United States, I buried my face in the neck of a turquoise piñata shaped like a turtle and said, "Mexico, Mexico, Mexico," over and over again. We caught the little wooden ball in the cup. We flipped the snake out of its box. We signed up for Spanish. Someday we would go there again.

And so I went back and back, over the years, as so many people who fall under the spell of Mexico have done, to find the gladiolas and tuberoses bundled in flower stalls, and small girls with tight new braids and freshly pressed school uniforms striding with book bags to school in the mornings, and Kickapoo Indians dancing in a circle twenty miles from any paved road, and the old man in the black suit in Matehuala who handed me a red carnation as I passed him then folded his hands and closed his eyes, and the graceful cactus fences, and the grinning little boys who know all the best shortcuts to any local destination, and Chamulan Indians lining up full Coke bottles as offerings in the churches of San

Cristóbal de las Casas, and the runaway horses in the mountains near Múzquiz, and the traffic of Mexico City which gives new flesh to a word like faith, and the secret emerald pools you have to hike to, and blue bowls of sliced papaya with lime, and elaborate gravestones shaped like castles, and the organ-grinder with his monkey on the Zona Rosa, and cities that climb slopes and curl into valleys, and the unforgettable photographs of Manuel Álvarez Bravo on his own table in his own house, and the magnificent museums and church bells and fiestas and fireworks and mercados. And I know I have seen only a tiny corner of all there is, just as the poems and stories in this book represent a small but important bit of the spectacular richness which is Mexican literature.

A Mexican artist friend says Mexico has always been a country of the spirit, a country where miracles feel close and possible, a country of passionate color and deep ties. In these days when "trade" is an amplified word, with the images of appliances and factories and skills flying back and forth across a border, I prefer to imagine cultures trading invisible riches. The stories and songs and ripe images of Mexico are a gift to our lives and hearts.

Now I live in one of the most Mexican of U.S. cities, in an inner-city neighborhood where no dinner table feels complete without a dish of *salsa* for gravity, and the soft air hums its double tongue. For some, this may not qualify me to gather writings of a culture not in my blood. I suggest that blood be bigger than what we're born with, that blood keep growing and growing as we live; otherwise how will we become true citizens of the world? For twenty years, working as a visiting writer in dozens of schools in my city and elsewhere, I have carried poems by writers of many cultures into classrooms, feeling the large family of voices linking human experience. We have no borders when we read.

Hopefully this gathering will serve as an invitation to further discoveries. Some of the writers in this collection are names well known and legendary— José Juan Tablada, Rosario Castellanos, and Octavio Paz among them. Others belong to a younger generation of voices. A few are teenagers, and at least one, Jesús Carlos Soto Morfín, is a child himself. While some of the included selections were originally written for a younger audience, many were not at all, but have been chosen for their ageless appeal. The artwork, collected through galleries, open invitations to art schools and institutions in Mexico, and word of mouth, represents a delicious spectrum of artists currently living and working in Mexico. A number of writers and artists included here have never published their work in the United States before. While we have presented Spanish originals of poems and stories, we have chosen to omit the original texts of poems first written in the less-widely spoken Tzotzil or Tzeltal languages. We have included one only as a sample. (See: "I Am a Peach Tree," p. 92.)

I hope you will find friends in this collection, and that their voices will travel with you. *Bienvenidos,* welcome! And particular thanks to the translators and advisors for this volume, especially Eliot Weinberger, Reginald Gibbons, Judith Infante, Joan Darby Norris, Tita Valencia, Mary Guerrero Milligan, John Igo, Christopher Johnson, Robert M. Laughlin, Oralia Cortés, Jennifer Clement, W. S. Merwin, Paulette Jiles, and Alberto Blanco. And again, an enormous debt of gratitude to my editor Virginia Duncan, to art director Christy Hale, to assistant editor Andrea Schneeman, and to editorial assistant Michael Nelson, who make books like this possible.

NAOMI SHIHAB NYE
San Antonio, Texas

PEOPLE

"Rub the Leaves in Your Hands"

La semilla (*The Seed*), José Jesús Chán Guzmán

Árbol de limón

Si te subes a un árbol de limón
siente la corteza
con tus rodillas y pies,
huele sus flores blancas,
talla las hojas
entre tus manos.
Recuerda,
el árbol es mayor que tú
y tal vez encuentres cuentos
entre sus ramas.

JENNIFER CLEMENT

Lemon Tree

If you climb a lemon tree
feel the bark
under your knees and feet,
smell the white flowers,
rub the leaves
in your hands.
Remember,
the tree is older than you are
and you might find stories
in its branches.

JENNIFER CLEMENT
Translated by Consuelo de Aerenlund

Barcos

1

Un poema es un barco de madera
hecho con tus propias manos:
es frágil, es pequeño,
pero te puede llevar tan lejos
como quiera el viento.

Un poema es un barco de madera
para viajar poco a poco,
y llegar hasta una isla lejana
y quedarte a vivir en ella
para siempre.

2

Un poema es un barco de papel
hecho con tus propias palabras:
toda tu vida cabe en el hueco
que dejan sus pliegues,
y sus colores.

Un poema es un barco de papel
para echarlo a navegar
en el estanque de tus días
y en la alberca nocturna
de tus mejores sueños.

3

Un niño es un barquito de madera:
sus remos son sus manos,
sus velas, su cabeza.

Una niña es un barquito de papel:
su forma es la mitad de una estrella
y su reflejo es la otra mitad.

4

La vida es un barco de madera
a la deriva de un sueño…
pero es también el agua donde flota
y el viento que lo mueve
y la imaginación que lo provoca.

La vida es un barco de papel…
pero es también el jardín triste
y los cristales manchados del estanque
donde se refleja el mundo
con sus respectivas sombras.

ALBERTO BLANCO

Boats

1

A poem is a boat built of wood
and made by your own hands:
it's fragile, it's small,
but it can carry you as far
as the wind wants.

A poem is a boat built of wood
to drift with the flow,
until you come to a remote island
and decide to live there
forever.

2

A poem is a paper boat
made of your own words:
everything in your life fits
in the spaces formed by its folds
and its colors.

A poem is a paper boat
to set sailing across
the lake of your days
and the nighttime pond
of your fondest dreams.

3

A boy is a small boat made of wood:
his oars are his hands,
the sails, his mind.

A girl is a small boat made of paper;
her shape is half a star
and her reflection the other part.

4

Life is a boat built of wood
sheltered by a dream…
but it's the water, too, where it floats,
and wind that sweeps it along,
and imagination that propels it.

Life is a paper boat…
but it's also a sad garden
and scarred crystals in a small lake
that reflect our globe
with all its shadows.

ALBERTO BLANCO
Translated by Judith Infante

El cabalista

Abraham el Cabalista sentó a los niños a su alrededor en un círculo de luz.
Les enseñó a dibujar las letras.
"La primera es la A, en cuyo trazo están todas las letras; y en cuyo sonido está toda la música. Si aprendéis a dibujar la A poseeréis los secretos del mundo".
Eso les dijo Abraham el Cabalista a los niños sentados en un círculo de luz y bajo los árboles de la Creación.

ANGELINA MUÑIZ-HUBERMAN

The Cabalist*

Abraham, the Cabalist, sat the children down around him in a circle of light.
He taught them to draw letters.
"The first of them is A; any letter can be made from its lines, and its sound encompasses every bit of music. If you learn to draw the letter A, you will possess all the world's secrets."
This is what Abraham, the Cabalist, told the children seated in a circle of light under Creation's tree of knowledge.

ANGELINA MUÑIZ-HUBERMAN
Translated by Christine Deutsch

*Cabalist—someone skilled in mysterious arts

Eva (Eve), Mario Rangel

Las preguntas de Natalia

Cuando dices ÁRBOL
¿cómo haces para ver
raíces hundidas en la tierra
o follajes que cuelgan
como una cabellera?

Cuando dices PEZ
¿qué ves?
¿Garabatos de luz
veloces como rayos?

Ah, palabras abiertas,
palabras que transforman
vocales en imágenes reales.

¿Quién estuvo en contra
de llamarle lengua a la vaca
y vaca a la piedra?

¿Quién les puso su nombre a las cosas?

Desconocidas voces
trajeron de oriente
hermosas palabras que empiezan con AL:
Almendra
Almíbar
Almeja
Almena
y a la estrella Aldebarán.

Después,
¿quién cambió las cosas del tablero?
¿quién creyó ver
en el cielo un velo extendido
sobre el mar?

¿Quién le dio al león
su nombre de rugido
y al perico su nombre parlanchín?

¿Y al puerco espín?
¿Quién le dio su doble nombre?
¿Quién le dio al oso
su nombre-pesadez?
¿Quién crees?

Que alguien diga
parado en su pradera
quién llamó a ese árbol
con su nombre de palmera.

Tu voz: golpe al oído.

Como un abracadabra
devuelve a la palabra
su último sentido.

MYRIAM MOSCONA

Natalia's Questions

When you say TREE
how can you make someone see
roots burrowing in the ground
or foliage that swings
like a ponytail?

When you say FISH
what do you see?
Scribblings of light
quick as waves?

Ah, open words,
words that change
a vowel into a picture.

Who was it who didn't want
to call the cow *tongue*
and the rock *cow?*

Who named things?

From the East
unknown voices brought
beautiful words beginning with AL:
ALMENDRA*
ALMÍBAR**
ALMEJA+
ALMENA++
and the star ALDEBARÁN.

Then,
who moved things off the page?
Who believed he saw in the sky
a veil spread out
over the sea?

Who gave to the lion
a name that roars
and to the parrot
one that's chatty?

And the porcupine?
Who gave him his double name?
Who gave the bear
his heavy name?
Whom do you think?

And can someone say
standing beside it
who called this tree
palm?

Your voice: a shock to the ear.

Like an abracadabra
gives back to the word
its final meaning.

MYRIAM MOSCONA
Translated by Judith Infante

*Almendra—almond
**Almíbar—sweet syrup
+Almeja—clam
++Almena—architectural frills

de **Duración**	*from* **Duration**
Te hablaré un lenguaje de piedra	I will speak to you in stone-language
(Respondes con un monosílabo verde)	(answer with a green syllable)
Te hablaré un lenguaje de nieve	I will speak to you in snow-language
(Respondes con un abanico de abejas)	(answer with a fan of bees)
Te hablaré un lenguaje de agua	I will speak to you in water-language
(Respondes con una canoa de relámpagos)	(answer with a canoe of lightning)
Te hablaré un lenguaje de sangre	I will speak to you in blood-language
(Respondes con una torre de pájaros)	(answer with a tower of birds)
OCTAVIO PAZ	OCTAVIO PAZ
	Translated by Denise Levertov

Ante la puerta	*At the Door*
Gentes, palabras, gentes.	People, words, people.
Dudé un instante:	I hesitated:
la luna arriba, sola.	up there the moon, alone.
OCTAVIO PAZ	OCTAVIO PAZ
de "Riprap"	Translated by Muriel Rukeyser
	from "Riprap"

Visión	*Vision*
Me vi al cerrar los ojos:	I saw myself when I shut my eyes:
espacio, espacio	space, space
donde estoy y no estoy.	where I am and am not.
OCTAVIO PAZ	OCTAVIO PAZ
de "Riprap"	Translated by Muriel Rukeyser
	from "Riprap"

Niño adorando al sol (*Child Adoring the Sun*), Julio López Segura

de *Coleadas*

Y quien dice monte
Dice varios montes:
La m de monte es dos montes,
La n de monte otro monte, otra vez;
El sol de la o entre estos montes
Asciende y deslumbra a los tres.

Y esto es lo que ocurre con viento:
La o jala siempre a la v.
La o es la boca del viento,
Y el viento va al viento y el viento
Se lleva a la rama de v.

En viento, tres cosas resisten
Al jalón del viento: la i, firme faro
Con e: cadena legada a sus pies;

El monte de n, recio aunque pelado,
Y la t: la torre desde donde miro
La vida que gira: derecho y revés.

LUIS MIGUEL AGUILAR

from *Wags*

...whoever says mountain
Says various mountains;
The m of mountain is two mountains,
The two n's are mountains, again;
The sunny o between these mountains
Rises and dazzles all four.

And this is what happens with windy:
The y always pulls the d.
The i is the eye of the storm,
And the wind blows in the wind
And the wind carries off the branch of the n.

In wind, three things resist
The force of the gale: the i, firm lighthouse
With the anchor of w chained to its base;

The mountain of n, strong although barren,
And the d: the deck from where I overlook
The life that swings: to and fro.

LUIS MIGUEL AGUILAR
Translated by Joan Darby Norris

de *Refranes*

EN EL MODO DE PEDIR
ESTÁ EL DAR.

MARGARITA ROBLEDA MOGUEL

from *Proverbs*

THE WAY YOU ASK
IS THE WAY YOU WILL RECEIVE.

MARGARITA ROBLEDA MOGUEL
Translated by Mary Guerrero Milligan

Marinero

Madre,
  ¿Lo sabías?

  Al arrullarme decidías
  mi vocación de marinero.

ALBERTO FORCADA

Sailor

Mother,
   Do you know?

My calling to the sea came
when you sang me to sleep.

ALBERTO FORCADA
Translated by Judith Infante

Despertar

Con voz arpónica me despierta mamá;
brillante y coleando me descama,
me cocina, me alhaja de cuadernos
y me avienta a los dientes numerados
de las Matemáticas.

ALBERTO FORCADA

Waking

With a harpoon voice my mother wakes me;
she scales me, shimmering and twitching my
  tail,
she cooks me and garnishes me with notebooks,
then casts me out to the numbered teeth
of Mathematics.

ALBERTO FORCADA
Translated by Judith Infante

La palabra

sale de la pluma
como el conejo del sombrero de un mago
astronauta que se sabe sola y sin peso
  suspendida en una línea
en el espacio

MANUEL ULACIA

The Word

comes out from the pen
like a rabbit from a magician's hat
astronaut who knows itself alone and weightless
  suspended on a line
in space

MANUEL ULACIA
Translated by Jennifer Clement

Día de lluvia (Rainy Day), Carmen Esquivel

La plaza

En la plaza
el asfalto descansa,
toma vacaciones,
se vuelve pista de patinaje,
danzan las bicicletas,
beben los teporochos.

Hijos de papá,
con sus mamás,
salen de misa,

los gorriones, gorrones,
disfrutan del festín
de las palomas;
pájaros de postín,
aves de cofia blanca.

El kiosko es un tíovivo
injertado en estatua,
un carrusel anquilosado
al que un día los caballitos
abandonaron.

La fuente en la plaza
es una palmera de agua,
la palmera una fuente;
la fuente y la palmera
son dos primas hermanas.

Las campanas de la iglesia
llaman a misa,
las del carrito de helados
muevan a risa.

No transcurre, se tiende
al sol la plaza,
me gusta este suelo común,
donde la gente descansa.

En la plaza todos se miran,
nadie se ofende,
se miran los edificios,
las banderas,
la gente.

The Plaza

In the plaza
the pavement has a rest,
takes a vacation,
becomes a skating rink,
bicycles dance,
the winos drink.

Daddy's children,
with their mamas,
come out of Mass,

the sparrows,
scroungers,
enjoy the pigeons' banquet;
swanky show-offs,
birds with white coifs.

The bandstand is a merry-go-round
grounded as a statue,
a carousel so old-fashioned
that one day the little horses
ran away.

The fountain in the plaza
is a palm tree of water,
the palm tree is a fountain;
the fountain and the palm tree
are two first cousins.

The church bells
call the people to Mass,
the bells on the ice cream cart
make the people laugh.

Time stops, the plaza stretches out
in the sun.
I like this place we share,
where people relax.

In the plaza everyone looks at each other,
no one minds,
the buildings,
the flags,
the people look at each other.

En la plaza se achatan	The plaza flattens
las puntas de las calles;	the tips of the streets;
las calles son agudas,	the streets are sharp,
la plaza es grave.	the plaza is solemn.
En el charco navega	In the puddle sails
una pluma de paloma,	the feather of a pigeon,
por la nube un avión,	an airplane through a cloud,
por la plaza una góndola.	a gondola through the plaza.
Gana cielo la plaza,	The plaza takes on the sky,
abre su ser al vuelo.	opens itself to flight.
La nube se detiene	The cloud stills
al verse reflejada	when it sees its own reflection
en el agua estancada	in the calm water
de la plaza.	of the plaza.
Bulle la plaza	The plaza bubbles
esas aguas tranquilas	these peaceful waters
hierven de niños y buñuelos,	simmering with children and fritters,
de globos y cornetas,	balloons and paper horns,
los cuetes suben al cielo	firecrackers go up in the sky
devolviéndole los truenos	returning thunderclaps
y una lluvia de luz	and a rain of light
amenaza el avión	threatens the airplane
que absurdamente vuela	that is silly to be flying
el 15 de septiembre,	on the 15th of September*
cuando todos deben estar en tierra.	when everyone should be on land.
Al día siguiente	The next day
la plaza es la misma de siempre:	the plaza is the same as always:
las palomas se reponen del susto	perched on the bandstand's eagle
de las luces y los cuetes	or on the hero's head,
sobre el águila del kiosco	the pigeons recover from the fright
o en la cabeza del héroe.	of lights and firecrackers.
Esos perros callejeros	Those street dogs
son unos mendigos habituales,	are regular beggars
ven con distancia	looking askance
(como los adultos a los niños)	(like grownups at children)
a esos otros	at other dogs
que libres por fin de la correa	that, finally free of their leashes
trotan y juegan con el agua;	trot and play in the water;

*September 15—Mexico's Independence Day

24

el cilindrero va por la plaza
con su música a cuestas,

en la fuente los niños
descubren el idioma:
antes que papá y mamá
con sus pequeñas manos sumergidas
dicen: "agua, agua".

La plaza es muy antigua:
sus abuelos en esta misma fuente,
oyendo el mismo rumor,
pronunciaron por primera vez
esta palabra.

ANTONIO DELTORO

the organ-grinder wanders through the plaza
with his music on his back,

in the fountain children
discover language:
before Papa and Mama
holding their little hands under,
they say, "Water, water."

The plaza is very ancient:
at this very fountain, their grandparents,
hearing the same burbling,
said this word
for the first time.

ANTONIO DELTORO
Translated by C. M. Mayo

Las mamás con bebé

Las mamás con bebé necesitan
de alguien que las duerma
les cuente un cuento
les prometa una fiesta
les cuelgue serpentinas
les regale paletas.

Las mamás con bebé necesitan
que les digan lo bonitas que son
con berrinche y sin él,
y cuando el bebé se enferma
o no quiere dormir
las mamás con bebé necesitan
un duende que les dé una cerveza
un hada que les haga masaje
un príncipe que les ponga su pijama
una tacita de sopa caliente
un pizarrón en blanco y a color
donde quepa un arco iris
un gran signo de interrogación
una varita mágica
un columpio, un volantín
un unicornio
una doncella encantada
que no ha tenido bebé
y a quien hay que contarle
todo lo que le espera
y decirle al final un buen final
como que, después de todo,
la mamá con bebé no se cambia
por una doncella encantada.

GUADALUPE MORFÍN

Mothers with a Baby

Mothers with a baby need
someone to sing them to sleep
to tell them a story
promise them a party
drape them in paper streamers
give them a candy.

A mother with a baby needs
someone to tell her how pretty she is
smelly or not
and when the baby gets sick
and won't go to sleep
the mother with a baby needs
an elf to bring her a beer
a fairy to give her a massage
a prince who will dress her in pajamas
a cup of hot soup
a blackboard that will hold a rainbow
and a chalk
a big question mark
a magic wand
a swing, a kite
a unicorn
an enchanted maiden
who has never had a baby
and the one who must be told
what's in store for her,
who must be told that finally, finally,
even after everything,
the mother with a baby would never change
places with an enchanted maiden.

GUADALUPE MORFÍN
Translated by Judith Infante

Allí había una niña

Allí había una niña.
En las hojas del plátano un pequeño
hombrecito dormía un sueño.
En un estanque, luz en agua.
Yo contaba un cuento.

Mi madre pasaba interminablemente
alrededor nuestro.
En el patio jugaba
con una rama un perro.
El sol —qué sol, qué lento—
se tendía, se estaba quieto.

Nadie sabía qué hacíamos,
nadie, qué hacemos.
Estábamos hablando, moviéndonos,
yendo de un lado a otro,
las arrieras, la araña, nosotros, el perro.
Todos estábamos en la casa,
pero no sé por qué. Estábamos. Luego el
    silencio.

Ya dije quién contaba un cuento.
Eso fue alguna vez porque recuerdo
que fue cierto.

JAIME SABINES

There Once Was a Girl

There once was a girl.
In the banana leaves a tiny
little man was dreaming a dream.
In a pond, light in water.
I was telling a tale.

My mother walked endlessly
around us.
In the patio a dog
played with a branch.
The sun—what a sun, how slow—
stretched itself, being quiet.

No one knew what we were doing,
no one, what we did.
We were talking, moving about,
going from one side to another,
the leaf cutter ants, the spider, the dog, and us.
We were all in the house,
but I don't know why. We were there. Then
    the silence.

I already said who was telling a tale.
That happened once because I remember
it was true.

JAIME SABINES
Translated by Joan Darby Norris and Barry Norris

Canicas

En el patio
juego a las canicas,
y una grande y naranjada
rueda detrás de una maceta de azaleas.
En la obscura sombra de la planta
encuentro dos arañas negras
y un pedazo de caramelo azul.

JENNIFER CLEMENT

Marbles

In the patio
I play with marbles,
and a large, orange one rolls
behind a pot of azaleas.
In the plant's dark shade
I find two black spiders
and a piece of blue candy.

JENNIFER CLEMENT
Translated by Consuelo de Aerenlund

Piñata

En la noche,
mientras dormíamos,
la piñata del cumpleaños se
cayó del árbol
como fruta demasiado madura
y tiró todos los dulces.
Nos dio mucho gusto
no tener que romperla
pues era un león amarillo
con sombrero verde.

JENNIFER CLEMENT

Piñata

In the night,
while we were asleep,
the birthday piñata
fell out of the tree
like an overripe fruit,
spilling all the candy.
We were happy
we did not have to break it
as it was a yellow lion
in a green hat.

JENNIFER CLEMENT
Translated by Consuelo de Aerenlund

En la plata

1

La más pequeña estrella adentro de mí
fue fraccionada en dos
para ella.

2

En los oscuros dísticos
cimientos de catedrales de átomos,
en el panal de cada célula
y molécula elevada al cubo,
en la plata de mi cuerpo
mi gemela está ausente
pero está.

3

Si aún la tuviera a mi lado,
ella podría recoserme
así como yo vuelvo a coser mi ropa vieja
para quitarle los años.

4

Si ella estuviera aquí,
nos pondríamos sombreros de paja
y nos iríamos a la feria.
Nos subiríamos al carrusel
22 veces.

JENNIFER CLEMENT

In the Silver

1

The smallest star in me
was split in two
for her.

2

In the dark couplets,
cathedrals of atoms,
in the honeycomb of every cell
and cubed molecule,
in the silver of my body
my twin is missing
and she is there.

3

If she were still beside me
she could sew me up,
as I sew the age
out of old clothes.

4

We would wear straw hats,
if she were here,
and go to the fair.
We'd ride the carousel
22 times.

JENNIFER CLEMENT
Translated by Consuelo de Aerenlund

untitled, Felipe Dávalos

El lápiz poeta

Era una vez un lápiz que quería escribir
poemas pero no tenía punta. Un día un niño
le metió un sacapuntas, y en lugar de punta
le salió un río.

JESÚS CARLOS SOTO MORFÍN

The Poet Pencil

Once upon a time a pencil wanted to write
poetry but it didn't have a point. One day a boy
put it into the sharpener, and in place of a point,
a river appeared.

JESÚS CARLOS SOTO MORFÍN
Translated by Judith Infante

de *Muro de lamentaciones*

Soy hija de mí misma.
De mi sueño nací. Mi sueño me sostiene.

No busquéis en mis filtros más que mi
  propia sangre
ni remontéis los ríos para alcanzar mi origen.

En mi genealogía no hay más que una palabra:
Soledad.

ROSARIO CASTELLANOS

from *The Wailing Wall*

I am my own daughter.
I was born from my own dream. My dream
  keeps me going.

Don't go looking for my springs anywhere but
  in my own blood,
and don't try to follow a river upstream back
  to my beginning.

In my family tree there's just one word:
Alone.

ROSARIO CASTELLANOS
Translated by Judith Infante

Canción de mayo

Eucaliptos encendidos, sombras:
    las mujeres lavan ropa. Pájaros
que cantan frente a la ventana.
    Las voces ascienden con el humo
de los coches, los ojos arden,
    el viento descorre las cortinas.
Un cielo lleno de nubes blancas
    es una cama con sábanas limpias.

ALBERTO BLANCO

Song for May

Glowing eucalyptos,* shadows:
    women washing clothes. Birds
that sing at my window.
    Voices rise with the smoke
from cars, eyes burn,
    the wind pulls back the curtains.
A sky covered by white clouds
    is a bed with clean sheets.

ALBERTO BLANCO
Translated by Judith Infante

Lavanderas del Grijalva

Pañuelo del adiós,
camisa de la boda,
en el río, entre peces
jugando con las olas.

Como un recién nacido
bautizado, esta ropa
ostenta su blancura
total y milagrosa.

Mujeres de la espuma
y el ademán que limpia,
halladme un río hermoso
para lavar mis días.

ROSARIO CASTELLANOS

Washerwomen at the Grijalva**

Handkerchief of good-bye,
wedding shirt,
in the river, among the fish
playing with the waves.

Like the baptism
of a newborn baby, these clothes
show off the whitest gleam,
complete and miraculous.

Women of foam and spray
and the movements that clean,
find for me a beautiful river
where I can wash my days.

ROSARIO CASTELLANOS
Translated by Judith Infante

*eucalyptos—eucalyptus trees
**Grijalva—a river in the state of Chiapas, Mexico

Pasajera

La luna es sólo
polvo en las cortinas,

Nubes azules
en el espejo del cuarto.

Cuando se mira
se pone triste y canta:

Su voz conduce
la sombra de los gatos.

ALBERTO BLANCO

In Passing

The moon is only
dust in the curtains.

Blue clouds
in the mirror of the room.

When she looks at herself
she feels sad and sings:

Her voice guides
a cat's shadow.

ALBERTO BLANCO
Translated by Judith Infante

Alba última

Tus cabellos se pierden en el bosque,
tus pies tocan los míos.
Dormida eres más grande que la noche
pero tu sueño cabe en este cuarto.
¡Cuánto somos qué poco somos!
Afuera pasa un taxi
con su carga de espectros.
El río que se va
    siempre
está de regreso.

¿Mañana será otro día?

OCTAVIO PAZ

Last Dawn

Your hair lost in the forest,
your feet touching mine.
Asleep you are bigger than the night,
but your dream fits within this room.

How much we are who are so little!
Outside a taxi passes
with its load of ghosts.
The river that runs by
    is always
running back.

Will tomorrow be another day?

OCTAVIO PAZ
Translated by Eliot Weinberger

Andrea

Andrea colibrí
salió al jardín
y danzó con el sol
del mediodía.
Cargó de flores
sus manos pequeñitas
se trepó a la mesa
y colocó su ofrenda
en un jarrón.
Andrea colibrí
nació en el sol
de nuestro mediodía
y puso a danzar
en el jardín
mi corazón.

GUADALUPE MORFÍN

Andrea

Andrea hummingbird
went into the garden
at noontime
and danced with the sun.
Her small hands filled
with flowers, she climbed
upon the table and arranged
her offering in a vase.
Andrea hummingbird
was born in the sun
of our noon
and began to dance
in the garden
of my heart.

GUADALUPE MORFÍN
Translated by Judith Infante

Serenata mexicana (Mexican Serenade), Rodolfo Morales

La nieta gitana

para Hattie

Tú tocas acordes gitanos,
  "¡Ay, Cielito Lindo!"
en la guitarra de listones coronada
la que guardo colgada del candelabro
si no vienes a merendar.

Tú eres mi nieta
soy de tu raza gitana
y por eso la cantamos al perro
y al gato lo asustamos
con el *clac* de mis castañuelas.

Yo soy tu abuela gitana
la que se divierte con palabras
la que te regala una libélula atada con hilo
para servirte de helicóptero privado,
y para tus calcetines, olorosos hechizos
de chícharo en flor, y cascabeles de víbora
para tu lonchera.

En la próxima noche lunera
cazaremos renacuajos
y cuando se vuelvan ranas
nos enseñarán sus acuáticos bailes,
los que bailan los gitanos allá en
  Chapultepéc
mientras le cantamos al perro
y al gato lo asustamos
con el *clac* de mis castañuelas.

MARTHA BLACK JORDAN

The Gypsy Granddaughter

for Hattie

You are strumming gypsy chords,
  "Ay, Cielito Lindo!"
on the ribbon-festooned guitar
that usually hangs from the chandelier
unless you come to tea.

You are my granddaughter
I am your gypsy kind
so we sing to the dog
and frighten the cat
with the click of my castanets.

I am your gypsy grandmother
the one who plays with words
who gives you a dragonfly tied to a thread
as your personal helicopter,
fragrant charms to put in your socks
like sweet pea petals and rattles of snakes
for your pencil box.

Next moonlight, we'll fish for tadpoles
and when they turn into frogs
they'll teach us their gypsy water dance,
the one they dance in Chapultepec*,
while we sing to the dog
and frighten the cat
with the clack of my castanets.

MARTHA BLACK JORDAN
Translated by the author

*Chapultepec—a huge public park containing a lake in
  Mexico City

Ombligo

Como los globos
que flotan en las fiestas,
tengo, para no desinflarme,
un nudo en el estómago.

ALBERTO FORCADA

Belly Button

Like the balloons
that float at parties,
I have a knot on my belly
so I won't go flat.

ALBERTO FORCADA
Translated by Judith Infante

Suéter

Abuela,
tengo frío;
téjeme a mí también
unas arrugas.

ALBERTO FORCADA

Sweater

Grandmother,
I'm cold;
can you knit me
some wrinkles?

ALBERTO FORCADA
Translated by Judith Infante

Y el niño un barco

Había una vez un barco
chiquito, tan chiquito,
que no podía navegar.
Pasaron una, dos, tres,
cuatro semanas, y el barquito…

"Parezco barco", dicen que dijo
unos días antes
de que saliera su niño
desde adentro de ella misma,
    su propio ombligo.

Ahora es una mujer que juega
    con su hijo,
como si ella fuera el agua
y el niño un barco que no naufraga
aunque se hunda,
porque estuviera hecho
de lo mismo que el agua
y las invenciones que hacen los niños
    cuando juegan.

RAÚL BAÑUELOS

And the Child a Boat

Once there was a little boat,
so small,
it couldn't even sail.
One, two, three,
four weeks passed and the little boat…

"I look like a boat," they say she said
some days before
her child would be born
from within her,
    her own center.

Now she is a woman who plays
    with her son,
as if she were water
and the child is a boat that doesn't perish
even though it sinks,
because he too is made of water
and the inventions of children
    when they play.

RAÚL BAÑUELOS
Translated by Joan Darby Norris

Naranjada

Mañana partida,
los gajos de nubes
dejan caer su semilla.
La naranja de sol,
muda de ropa.

LUIS MEDINA GUTIÉRREZ

Orangeade

At dawn
the cloud sections
drop their seed.

The sunny orange
changes clothes.

LUIS MEDINA GUTIÉRREZ
Translated by Joan Darby Norris

Nieve

Mi madre
me compró
una luna.

La pedí
de limón.

ALBERTO FORCADA

Snow Cone

My mother
bought me
a moon.

I asked
for lemon.

ALBERTO FORCADA
Translated by Judith Infante

Canción de enero

La hora es fresca y los niños
   en la escuela con ansiedad aguardan
el perfil del carro de raspados:
   botellas de colores que confunden
con su cielo profundo la mirada.
   Soles, sueños del dulce principio...
el brillo de los rayos despierta
   en la nieve gris de los volcanes.

ALBERTO BLANCO

Song for January

The hour is cool and in class children
   anxiously keep watch
for the outline of the snow cone cart:
   bottles of color that confuse
one's gaze with the deep sky.
   Suns, dreams of sweet beginnings...
the sparkle of their rays awakens
   in the gray snow of volcanoes.

ALBERTO BLANCO
Translated by Judith Infante

Globo	Balloon

Allá va el globo:
se aleja y nos devuelve la distancia
Subirse a la azotea
y dejarlo escapar por puro gusto
es como abrir la puerta de una jaula

(Si alguno se nos fuga por descuido
lloramos su retiro anticipado
y su vuelo es tan corto,
nos parece tan previsible
y frágil su futuro
que por poco y podríamos
correr a rescatarlo)

Allá va el globo:
sobre techos y cables,
con el viento,
bautizando paisajes y miradas

EDUARDO HURTADO

There goes the balloon:
it gets away and gives us back the distance
To go up to the roof
and let it go just for fun
is like opening the door of a cage

(If one escapes by accident
we cry for its early retirement
and its flight is so short,
its future seems so predictable
and fragile
that we could almost run
to rescue it)

There goes the balloon:
over rooftops and cables,
with the wind,
baptizing landscapes and vistas

EDUARDO HURTADO
Translated by C. M. Mayo

Luna y sol juntos (Moon and Sun Together), Chan Kin Norris

Homenaje a una niña en su columpio

La niña blanca balancea su cuerpo feliz
borrándolo y pintándolo en la ráfaga del
  tiempo.

Su ave se acuesta en la espalda del paisaje
a esperar que se abra la puerta violeta
por donde ha de cruzar en su caballo alado.

Alguien desde lo alto conocerá su nombre
y la llamará con las voces del relámpago.
Aquí la Tierra la verá irse en silencio
como las flechas de los venados azules.

RAÚL ACEVES

Homage to a Girl in a Swing

The pale girl bounces her body happily
erasing and painting it in the gusts of time.

Her bird lies down on the landscape's spine
to await the opening of the purple door
through which she will cross on her winged
  horse.

Someone on high will know her name
and call her with the voices of lightning.
From here Earth will see her go silently
like the blue deer's arrows.

RAÚL ACEVES
Translated by Yvette Grutter and Joan Darby Norris

Balneario

La niña pregunta por el agua
corre con el salvavidas
brinca
la alberca estornuda

LUIS MEDINA GUTIÉRREZ

The Bathing Place

The girl greets the water
runs with her inner tube
jumps
the pool sneezes

LUIS MEDINA GUTIÉRREZ
Translated by Joan Darby Norris

Cautiva

Una alberca es renuente,
con sus manos crispadas de cloro,
azulmente amarrada a los bordes,
con su melena de silencio estancada,
es presa del guiño de los astros.

LUIS MEDINA GUTIÉRREZ

Captive

A pool is reluctant,
hands twitching from chlorine
tied bluely at its sides,
with its mane of silence
prisoner to the twinkling stars.

LUIS MEDINA GUTIÉRREZ
Translated by Joan Darby Norris

El día que dejó

El día que dejó
ecos en las cosas

el día que cantó
luz por sus bocas

pobre de oros
y oscuro ya

como león herido
que sangra por el horizonte

se arrodilla sobre los fresnos
y el polvo

HOMERO ARIDJIS

The Day That Left

The day that left
echoes in things

the day that sang
light through their mouths

beggar of gold
dark now

like a wounded lion
bleeding on the horizon

it kneels
on the ash-trees and dust

HOMERO ARIDJIS
Translated by Eliot Weinberger

El carrito de Monchito

Monchito Monchito tenía su carrito tan grande tan grande como un elefante.

¿Como un elefante?
No.

Monchito Monchito tenía su carrito tan chico tan chico como una hormiguita.

¿Como una hormiguita?
No.

Monchito Monchito tenía su carrito tan lejos tan lejos como un helicóptero.

¿Como un helicóptero?
No.

Monchito Monchito tenía su carrito tan cerca tan cerca como una peca.

¿Como una peca?
No.

Monchito Monchito tenía su carrito tan suave tan suave como una almohada.

¿Como una almohada?
No.

Monchito Monchito tenía su carrito tan sabroso tan sabroso como un helado de fresa.

¿Como un helado de fresa?
No.

Monchito Monchito tenía su carrito tan duro tan duro como un martillo.

¿Como un martillo?
No.

Monchito Monchito tenía su carrito tan frío tan frío como un cubito de hielo.

¿Como un cubito de hielo?
No.

Monchito Monchito tenía su carrito tan cariñoso tan cariñoso como un oso panda.

¿Como un oso panda?
No.

Monchito Monchito tenía su carrito, que no estaba lejos ni cerca, no es sabroso ni suave, frío ni duro, ni siquiera cariñoso…

…pero el carrito que tiene Monchito, es el carrito más hermoso de todo el universo, porque es el carrito que tiene Monchito.

MARGARITA ROBLEDA MOGUEL

Monchito's Little Car

Monchito, Monchito had a car
as big, as big
as an elephant.

As an elephant?
No.

Monchito, Monchito had a car
as small, as small
as an ant.

As an ant?
No.

Monchito, Monchito had a car
as far away, as far away
as a helicopter.

As a helicopter?
No.

Monchito, Monchito had a car
as near, as near
as a freckle.

As a freckle?
No.

Monchito, Monchito had a car
as soft, as soft
as a pillow.

As a pillow?
No.

Monchito, Monchito had a car
as delicious, as delicious
as strawberry ice cream.

As strawberry ice cream?
No.

Monchito, Monchito had a car
as hard, as hard
as a hammer.

As a hammer?
No.

Monchito, Monchito had a car
as cold, as cold
as an ice cube.

As an ice cube?
No.

Monchito, Monchito had a car
as loving, as loving
as a panda bear.

As a panda bear?
No.

Monchito, Monchito had a car that wasn't
far away or near, delicious or soft,
cold or hard, not even loving…

but Monchito's car is the most
beautiful in all the universe
because it belongs to Monchito.

MARGARITA ROBLEDA MOGUEL
Translated by Mary Guerrero Milligan

Story of the Lazy Man and the Ants

A man was very lazy at working.
A man feels he will never be finished working.
A man slept at his work.
A man didn't work much every day.
A man only felt like working a little bit every day.
Every day a man sleeps at his work.
When his work grabs him he scratches his
    head a lot.
Every day a man is just yawning at his work.
There is the sun.
Went to see the lazy man.
When the sun gets to the lazy man
He finds him sleeping at his work.
The lazy man is crying through his nose in his
    sleep. He is snoring.
The sun says, "What a lazy man at his work!
    What a lot he sleeps!"
The sun grabbed dust in his hand.
Three times.
The sun threw handfuls of dust
Where the lazy man was sleeping.
The sun made the dust turn into ants.
Then the dust turned into ants.
The ants of earth fell onto the lazy man
Where he was sleeping.
The lazy man opened his eyes
Because of the ants.
The ants bit him and the bites hurt very
much.
The lazy man lost his sleep
Because of the ants.
The lazy man's laziness all went out of him
Because of the ants biting him.
Every day a man does not sleep at his work.
In fact there are many ants at his work.
Long ago the sun turned dust into ants
Because of a lazy man.
Now on earth there are many ants
Because of lazy men.

Mayan poem related by Santiago Mendes Zapata (Tenejapa)
Literal version from Tzeltal into Spanish
by Katherine B. Bransetter
Translated by W. S. Merwin

Homenaje a un jardín de hipocampos

En el acuario, mundo de paredes
    transparentes,
todos los habitantes nadaban silenciosos;
el único tumulto procedía de las burbujas
    de oxígeno.

Los pececillos multicolores en un recreo de
    entusiasmo escolar,
no se despintaban al jugar a la trais o a las
    escondidas.
(Al fin, niños del agua).

Entre corales y vegetaciones los hipocampos
    color de tierra
jugaban a ser colas enrolladas en espirales
    asombrosas
y cabecitas equinas de una mitología
    milagrosamente aquí.

A la hora de la danza se convertían en
    pequeñura grácil
que imantaba la mirada entregada al jardín,
desde su ser de agua nos relinchaban
    los caballitos de juguetería.

RAÚL ACEVES

Homage to a Sea Horse Garden

In the fish tank, world of transparent walls,
all inhabitants swam silently;
the only tumult came from the oxygen
    bubbles.

The schools of fish at recess did not lose
    their color
while playing hide and seek.
(Anyway, they were water kids.)

Among coral and vegetation, the earth-colored
    sea horses
twisted their tails in astonishing spirals,
little horse's heads in a miraculous mythology.

At the time of dancing, their graciousness
magnetically attracted gazes toward the garden
where, from their own watery beings,
    the little horses would neigh.

RAÚL ACEVES
Translated by Yvette Grutter

Objetos

Viven a nuestro lado,
los ignoramos, nos ignoran.
Alguna vez conversaron con nosotros.

OCTAVIO PAZ
de "Lección de cosa"

Objects

They live alongside us,
we do not know them, they do not know us.
But sometimes they speak with us.

OCTAVIO PAZ
Translated by Muriel Rukeyser
from "Object Lesson"

Homenaje a Frida y a Diego (Homage to Frida and Diego), Iliana Fuentes R.

Noche en la cocina

De su vaina salen los chícharos
rápidas sombras verdes
junto a una cuchara sola

HOMERO ARIDJIS

Night in the Kitchen

Peas come out of their pods
quick green shadows
by a single spoon

HOMERO ARIDJIS
Translated by Eliot Weinberger

Momento

Sobre la mesa
la luz recorre el pan
como si lo comiera

y recorrido
el pan queda entero

la sal la azucarera
dejan caer sus sombras
y no hay otra cosa

HOMERO ARIDJIS

Moment

Light examines the bread
on the table
as though it wanted to eat

and examined
the bread remains whole

the salt the sugar bowl
let their shadows fall
and there is nothing else

HOMERO ARIDJIS
Translated by Eliot Weinberger

Meteoro

Sobre la mesa
un vaso
se desmaya,
    rueda,
        cae.

Al estrellarse
contra el piso,
una galaxia
    nace.

ELÍAS NANDINO

Meteor

Upon the table
a glass
faints,
    rolls,
        falls.

Crashing
to the floor,
a galaxy
    is born.

ELÍAS NANDINO
Translated by Joan Darby Norris

La niña de los chocolates

Camina con sus sandalias
por la calzada una niñita.
Su cabellera es larga y negra
que se vuelve azul marino
de tanto brillo.

Lleva puesto un vestido verde
con siete flores en su pechera
y con su mano sostiene
una cajita de chocolates.

Sólo tiene seis años
y sueña con ir a la escuela
pero tiene que vender chocolates
y cuidar de sus hermanos.

Con sus hermanitos
y sus muñequitos, en el futuro,
hará un equipo de fútbol
pero antes irá por la calzada
con sus sandalias
vendiendo chocolates.

HUGO GARCÍA GONZÁLEZ

The Little Girl with Chocolates

A little girl in sandals
is walking on the avenue.
Her hair, so long and black,
shines and turns deep sea-blue.

She wears a green dress
with seven flowers
printed on the front
and carries a box of chocolates.

At six years old
school is her only dream
but she must sell her chocolates
and care for her brothers and sisters.

Someday she will play soccer on a team
with her brothers, sisters and dolls.
But for now she is selling chocolates
walking in sandals on the avenue.

HUGO GARCÍA GONZÁLEZ
Translated by the author

La libertad

Lo que yo más amo,
es la Libertad;
nunca, a un pajarito,
ni a nadie
se la he de quitar.

A. L. JÁUREGUI

Liberty

What I love the most
is freedom;
not from a bird,
nor from anyone,
shall I take it
away, ever.

A. L. JÁUREGUI
Translated by Angela de Hoyos

Mundo escondido

Es el lugar de las computadoras
y de las ciencias infalibles.
Pero de pronto te evaporas
—y creo en las cosas invisibles.

JOSÉ EMILIO PACHECO

Hidden World

It's the place of the computers
and the certain silences.
But suddenly you evaporate
—and I believe in the invisible.

JOSÉ EMILIO PACHECO
Translated by Joan Darby Norris

Agua nocturna

La noche de ojos de caballo que tiemblan
   en la noche,
la noche de ojos de agua en el campo dormido,
está en tus ojos de caballo que tiembla,
está en tus ojos de agua secreta.

Ojos de agua de sombra,
ojos de agua de pozo,
ojos de agua de sueño.

El silencio y la soledad,
como dos pequeños animales a quienes
   guía la luna,
beben en esos ojos,
beben en esas aguas.

Si abres los ojos,
se abre la noche de puertas de musgo,
se abre el reino secreto del agua
que mana del centro de la noche.

Y si los cierras,
un río te inunda por dentro,
avanza, te haré oscura:
la noche moja riberas en tu alma.

OCTAVIO PAZ

Water Night

Night with the eyes of a horse that trembles
    in the night,
night with eyes of water in the field asleep,
is in your eyes, a horse that trembles,
is in your eyes of secret water.

Eyes of shadow-water,
eyes of well-water,
eyes of dream-water.

Silence and solitude,
two little animals moon-led,
drink in your eyes,
drink in those waters.

If you open your eyes,
night opens, doors of musk,
the secret kingdom of the water opens
flowing from the center of the night.

And if you close your eyes,
a river fills you from within,
flows forward, darkens you:
night brings its wetness to beaches in
    your soul.

OCTAVIO PAZ
Translated by Muriel Rukeyser

EARTH and ANIMALS
"Impulse of Roots"

Canto de coyotes (Coyote Song), Julia López

Parque Morelos

Una mañana lavada
anuncia que vendrá la primavera
descendiendo entre ramas húmedas
descendiendo
por las primeras flores de las jacarandás

El gozo no está en la vida afuera
en la tristeza afuera
en las calles grises
ni en el humo
El gozo viene en la sangre
subiendo por las venas
la sangre nueva

El gozo se siente en la piel que besa el aire
y en el cabello ondeando al aire

El gozo está naciendo en las pupilas
plenas de ese verde brillante
mojado cubriendo el parque

ADRIANA DÍAZ ENCISO

Morelos Park

A washed morning
announces that spring will come
dropping down between damp branches
dropping down
through the first jacaranda flowers

Joy is not in the life outside
in the sadness outside
in the gray streets
nor in the smoke
Joy comes in the blood
rising up in the veins
new blood

Joy is felt in skin that kisses air
and in breeze-waving hair

Joy is being born in eyes
brimming with this brilliant wet
green covering the park

ADRIANA DÍAZ ENCISO
Translated by Brandel France de Bravo
and Naomi Shihab Nye

Pájaro carpintero

Pájaro carpintero,
picamadero,
cuánto me cobra usted
por un librero.

Maestro carpintero,
copete-rojo,
mondador de cortezas,
come-gorgojos,

cuánto por una cama
de buen encino,
cuánto por una silla
de puro pino.

Pájaro carpintero,
sacabocado,
cuánto por un trastero
bien cepillado.

Diga cuánto, maestro,
pico-de-acero,
porque me cante, cuánto,
buen carpintero.

Porque me cante, cuánto,
carpinterillo,
al compás de los golpes
de su martillo.

GILDA RINCÓN

The Woodpecker

Woodpecker,
woodpicker,
how much will you charge me
for a bookcase?

Mr. Woodpecker,
red crest,
peeler of bark,
grub eater,

how much for a bed
of good oak,
how much for a chair
of pure pine?

Woodpecker,
taker of mouthfuls,
how much for a cupboard
well-sanded?

Tell me how much, sir,
beak of steel,
how much would it be,
good carpenter?

Sing me the sum,
little carpenter,
at the pace of the beats
of your hammer.

GILDA RINCÓN
Translated by Joan Darby Norris and Chan Kin Norris

Patos

1

Patos en la mañana fría
resbalan sobre el hielo
tras el pan seco
que les echa una niña

2

Patos hambrientos
en la tarde
cruzan la calle
entre los coches

3

Patos en la noche
ateridos junto al canal helado
casi no mueven
las cabezas verdes

4

Patos al alba
duermen bajo la niebla
que cubre también al hombre
al perro y a la piedra

HOMERO ARIDJIS

Ducks

1

On cold mornings the ducks
slide across the ice
after the dry bread
thrown to them by the little girl

2

In the afternoon
the hungry ducks
cross the street
against the traffic

3

At night the ducks
nestle beside the frozen canal
they scarcely move
their green heads

4

At dawn the ducks
sleep beneath the mist
which covers the man
the dog and the stone alike

HOMERO ARIDJIS
Translated by Martha Black Jordan

La hechicera

Velos, gasas y tules adornan a la bella Alisa la Hechicera. No camina, sino que baila. No habla, sino que canta. Vuela por los aires y de sus manos caen todos los dones, las dichas y las flores para todos los niños de todos los rincones del mar, el valle y la montaña.

ANGELINA MUÑIZ-HUBERMAN

The Sorceress

Veils, gauzes, and fine sheer nets bedeck the lovely Alisa, the Sorceress. She doesn't walk, but rather dances. She does not speak, but rather sings. She flies through the air and from her hands fall all sorts of talents, joys and flowers for all those children living in even the tiniest corners of the seas, the valleys and the mountains.

ANGELINA MUÑIZ-HUBERMAN
Translated by Christine Deutsch

Mi conejo (My Rabbit), Iliana Fuentes R.

de *Homenaje a las islas galletas*

Las islas galletas no existen en el mapa.
¿Cómo podrían existir
     si son más reales que la geografía?

Me gustaría viajar a las islas galletas
     para comérmleas con cajeta,
o mejor para ver si de veras
     hay tres Marías y un solo mar verdadero.

Al mar iría si ahí estuviera María
     y una caja de islas yo compraría
si me aseguraran que contiene
     Marías de todas las islas.

Si como no, yo iría a las islas galletas
aungue tuviera que viajar en acuarela
     o litografía

RAÚL ACEVES

from *Homage to the Cookie Islands*

The Cookie Islands don't exist on any map.
How could they exist
     if they are more real than geography?

I would like to travel to the Cookie Islands
     to eat them with caramel sauce,
or better, to see if there
     really are three Marias* and only one true sea.

I would go to sea if Maria were there
     and I would buy one box of islands
if I were assured it contained
     Marias on every island.

Of course, I would go to the Cookie Islands
even if I had to travel into a watercolor or
     lithograph

RAÚL ACEVES
Translated by Christopher Johnson

Embrujo

Los árboles son pájaros hechizados.
No pueden despegar la pata del suelo.
Una y otra vez aletean con furia.
Se arrancan las plumas, sollozan.

¿Cómo romper el maleficio?
¿Qué palabras deberé pronunciar?

¿Cuántas veces tendré que besarlos?

ALBERTO FORCADA

Enchantment

The trees are birds bewitched.
They can't lift their feet from the ground.
Again and again they beat their wings
furiously, pluck at their feathers, weep.

How can I break this spell?
What words should I say?

How many times must I kiss them?

ALBERTO FORCADA
Translated by Judith Infante

*Marias—popular Mexican cookies

El cacto

Crece sobre sí mismo
como una llama

solitario en el llano
recoge el rayo de sol
la noche el trueno

casi arrancado por el viento
quemado y seco
da su flor

HOMERO ARIDJIS
de "Diario sin fechas"

Cactus

It grows on itself
like a flame

solitary on the plain
it gathers the sunrays
the night the thunderclap

almost uprooted by the wind
burnt and dry
it flowers

HOMERO ARIDJIS
Translated by Eliot Weinberger
from "Diary Without Dates"

A la orilla del agua

Gaviotas hambrientas
bajo la llovizna

blancas nadas
entre yerbas y grises

blanco vuelo
con las alas cerradas

gaviotas hambrientas
sobre el pasto lejanas

HOMERO ARIDJIS
de "Diario sin fechas"

At the Water's Edge

Hungry gulls
in the drizzle

white nothings
between grass and gray

white flight
with folded wings

hungry gulls
far-off on the meadow

HOMERO ARIDJIS
Translated by Eliot Weinberger
from "Diary Without Dates"

de *Versos de la ciudad*

Duerme la ciudad:
ángeles de piedra,
esqueletos de aire.
Lloverá,
un escalofrío
baja por el árbol.

RAMIRO LOMELÍ

from *Verses of the City*

The city sleeps:
angels of stone,
skeletons in the air.
It will rain,
a chill
creeps down the tree.

RAMIRO LOMELÍ
Translated by Joan Darby Norris

¿De dónde viene el polvo?

Guy preguntó a Jacinto Canek:
—¿De dónde viene, Jacinto, el polvo que se pega en las ventanas, en las imágenes, en los libros y en la tela de los retratos?

Jacinto Canek contestó:
—Como todo lo de la vida, niño Guy, viene de la tierra.

Guy replicó:
—No lo creo, Jacinto. El polvo que se pega en las ventanas, en las imágenes, en los libros y en la tela de los retratos, no viene de la tierra. Viene del viento. Es el viento mismo que muere de cansancio y de sed en el rincón de las cosas íntimas.

ERMILO ABREU GÓMEZ

Where Does the Dust Come From?

Guy asked Jacinto Canek, "Jacinto, where does the dust come from, the dust that clings to the windows, the saints, to the books, and the picture frames?"

Jacinto Canek replied, "As with everything in life, little Guy, it comes from the earth."

Guy replied, "I don't think so, Jacinto. The dust that clings to the glass on the windows, to the saints, that covers books and picture frames, does not come from the earth. It comes from the wind. It's the wind itself which dies tired and thirsty in the corner of close things."

ERMILO ABREU GÓMEZ
Translated by Judith Infante

La novia *(The Girlfriend)*, Julio Galán

María la de las dulces peras verdes

Con diecisiete años y mucha pena
Responde a mis palabras
Con risitas nerviosas
Dientes que se asemejan
A los de la blanca mazorca

Se sube el largo cabello a la coronilla
En un chongo doble
Que se mece, muy formal
Cuando hace el quehacer.

María teme las miradas directas
Sus ojillos de pepita de sandía
Se escurren
Como peces pequeños
Tratando de escapar

Con paso felino, silencioso
Se apura en su trabajo
Feliz
A pesar de la exigente Nana
Quien ha estado con nosotros desde
    hace siglos.

Del árbol de su rancho
Me trajo seis verdes peras.
Le dije a Nana que las hiciera en dulce
Pero María dijo ¡No! si cuecen la fruta
Seguro que el árbol morirá.

CONSUELO DE AERENLUND

Maria of the Sweet Green Pears

Seventeen and shy
she greets my words
with flustered giggles
teeth like
white maize kernels

Bunches up long hair on her crown
in a double topknot
that waves in stilted formality
as she goes about
her daily chores

Maria fears to meet any gaze
Her quick watermelon-seed eyes
dart about
like small fish
seeking to escape

With noiseless, catlike tread
she hurries through her work
happy
despite the presence of lemony Nana
who has been with us for ages

From her home tree
she brought six country pears
I told Nana to stew them but
Maria said oh no, if you cook its fruit
the tree will surely die

CONSUELO DE AERENLUND
Translated by the poet

63

Cofre de cedro

El hacha que taló
para siempre olorosa
y el árbol cautivado
con las entrañas rotas.

Aquí estás, bajo un techo,
en un rincón de alcoba
y te confían huéspedes
y tú, como que aceptas y reposas.

No vendas tu memoria
a la triste costumbre y a los años.
Nunca olvides el bosque
ni el viento ni los pájaros.

ROSARIO CASTELLANOS

The Cedar Chest

The ax that felled
forever the fragrance
and the tree taken
with its torso severed.

Now here you are, under a roof,
in the corner of a bedroom
and guests take you for granted
and you, you seem to accept it
    and to keep still.

Don't sell away your memory
to sad routines and to time.
Do not forget the woods
or the wind or the birds.

ROSARIO CASTELLANOS
Translated by Judith Infante

Panorama

Bajo de mi ventana, la luna en los tejados
y las sombras chinescas
y la música china de los gatos.

JOSÉ JUAN TABLADA

Under my window
Moon on the roofs
And the Chinese shadows
And the Chinese music of the cats

JOSÉ JUAN TABLADA
Translated by Eliot Weinberger

Los sapos

Trozos de barro,
por la senda en penumbra
saltan los sapos.

JOSÉ JUAN TABLADA

Mad lump bumped
    In the shadow
    Toad
    Tiptoed

JOSÉ JUAN TABLADA
Translated by Eliot Weinberger

Mesa de noche (Table of Night), Mario Rangel

The Three Suns

Long ago there were three suns.
There was no darkness. The suns took turns.
There was always day because of the three suns.

They traveled together. They went for a walk.
They went to look for fruits.
The two older brothers climbed a tree.
The younger brother stayed below.

"Give me some fruit," said the little brother. "Throw one down to me."
"Come on, climb up!" said the older brothers.
"I can't climb up. Throw some down!"

The fruits were thrown down, but just the chewings.
The little brother picked up the chewings and turned them into
hind legs and forelegs.
He buried them at the foot of the tree.
They turned into a gopher. It gnawed the roots to pieces.
The older brothers felt the tree moving.

"What are you doing, Xut?" asked the older brothers.
"I'm not doing anything. Eat your fruit."

The tree fell. Down came his mean older brothers.
Xut went home.

"Mother, I'm hungry! Give me six tortillas."

He went back and grabbed his older brothers.
Quickly he stuck noses and ears on them.
He made their noses and ears out of the six tortillas.
He turned one into a peccary*, the other into a pig.
The peccary ran away.
He caught it by the tail, but its tail came off.
It fled into the woods.

He drove the pig to his house.

"Mother, I've brought a pig. The pig is hungry. Let's fatten it up."
"All right," said his mother. "But where are your older brothers?"
"I don't know. They must be having a good time someplace," said Xut.

The first day she believed it.
Then his mother cried and cried. Her tears flowed.
Now the moon's light is faint at night.

ROMIN TERATOL
Translated from the Tzotzil by Robert M. Laughlin

*peccary—a grizzled, gregarious mammal resembling a pig

La manzana

Sabe a luz, a luz fría,
sí, la manzana.
¡Qué amanecida fruta
tan de mañana!

JOSÉ GOROSTIZA

The Apple

Yes, the apple tastes of light,
cold light.
That's it, the apple!
What a lively fruit
so much like morning!

JOSÉ GOROSTIZA
Translated by Joan Darby Norris and Judith Infante

La luna, un plátano

Un plátano se fue
de noche
en un avión

Desde entonces
se quedó pegado
en el cielo
y le llaman luna

JESÚS CARLOS SOTO MORFÍN

The Moon, a Banana

A banana left
at night
on a plane

Since then
he's been stuck
in the sky
and we call him moon

JESÚS CARLOS SOTO MORFÍN
Translated by Judith Infante

La oración en el huerto

En sus ojitos
había sueños
color de olivo.

MANUEL PONCE

The Prayer in the Orchard

In their little eyes
there were
olive colored dreams.

MANUEL PONCE
Translated by Joan Darby Norris

Sol de Monterrey

No cabe duda: de niño,
a mí me seguía el sol.
Andaba detrás de mí
como perrito faldero;
  despeinado y dulce,
  claro y amarillo:
  ese sol con sueño
  que sigue a los niños.

Saltaba de patio en patio,
se revolcaba en mi alcoba.
Aun creo que algunas veces
lo espantaban con la escoba.
Y a la mañana siguiente,
ya estaba otra vez conmigo,
  despeinado y dulce,
  claro y amarillo:
  ese sol con sueño
  que sigue a los niños.

  (El fuego de mayo
  me armó caballero:
  yo era el Niño Andante,
  y el sol, mi escudero.)

Todo el cielo era de añil;
toda la casa, de oro.
¡Cuánto sol se me metía
por los ojos!
Mar adentro de la frente,
a donde quiera que voy,
aunque haya nubes cerradas,
¡oh cuánto me pesa el sol!
¡Oh cuánto me duele, adentro,
esa cisterna de sol
que viaja conmigo!

Yo no conocí en mi infancia
sombra, sino resolana.—
Cada ventana era sol,
cada cuarto era ventanas.

Los corredores tendían
arcos de luz por la casa.
En los árboles ardían
las ascuas de las naranjas,
y la huerta en lumbre viva
se doraba.
Los pavos reales eran
parientes del sol. La garza
empezaba a llamear
a cada paso que daba.

Y a mí el sol me desvestía
para pegarse conmigo,
  despeinado y dulce,
  claro y amarillo:
  ese sol con sueño
  que sigue a los niños.

Cuando salí de mi casa
con mi bastón y mi hato,
le dije a mi corazón:
—¡Ya llevas sol para rato!—
Es tesoro —y no se acaba:
no se me acaba —y lo gasto.
Traigo tanto sol adentro
que ya tanto sol me cansa.—
Yo no conocí en mi infancia
sombra, sino resolana.

ALFONSO REYES

Monterrey Sun

No shadow of doubt; the sun
dogged me when I was a boy,
and pattered at my heels,
a toy dog trailing me;
   disheveled and soft,
   shining and golden,
   the sun that drowsily
   dogs small children.

It frisked in all the courtyards,
basking in my bedroom.
At times it seemed to me
they shooed it with a broom.
But on the following day,
it was treading on my heels;
   disheveled and soft,
   shining and golden,
   the sun that drowsily
   dogs small children.

   (I was dubbed a knight
   by the May fire.
   I was dubbed Boy-Errant,
   the sun became my squire.)

All the sky was indigo,
all the house was gold.
Oh how much sunlight filtered in
the lake between my eyes!
Sea inside my forehead,
wherever I may go,
if clouds are low, oh how much sun
weighs down on me like lead!
Oh how this pool of sun,
my traveling companion,
keeps wounding me inside!

As a child, I only
knew sunroom, I never knew shadow.
Each window was sun,
each room was windows.
In the house, the hallways
hung arches of sun.
The oranges burned
red coals on the boughs.
The orchard turned golden
with living sparks.
The peacocks were cousins
to the sun. And the heron
burst into tongues of flame
with each step it took.

The sun stripped off my clothes
to stick closer to my body;
   disheveled and soft,
   shining and golden,
   the sun that sleepily
   dogs small children.

When I went from my home
with my pack on my back,
I said to my heart,
"You've enough sun to last!
It's gold . . . and it doesn't run out!"
And I never exhaust it, whatever I spend!
But I start to grow tired
from the sun in my head . . .
In my childhood, I never
knew shadow, only sunroom.

ALFONSO REYES
Translated by Cheli Durán

69

Ni una nube

El sol se deslíe en viento de brasa.
—Niño Guy—dijo Canek—, ni una nube.
Si no llueve pronto, se perderán las cosechas.

Al día siguiente Guy encendió una hoguera y con ímpetu se puso a soplar con su boca y a aventar con las manos las columnas de humo que subían.

Canek le preguntó:
—¿Qué haces?

—Nubes, Jacinto, nubes.

ERMILO ABREU GÓMEZ

Not Even a Cloud

The sun slipped into the wind that burned like a coal. "Little Guy," said Jacinto Canek, "there's not a single cloud. If it doesn't rain soon, we'll lose our crops."

The next day Guy made a fire and forcefully began to blow on it with his mouth and fan the rising columns of smoke with his hands.

Canek asked him, "What are you making?"

"Clouds, Jacinto, clouds."

ERMILO ABREU GÓMEZ
Translated by Judith Infante

Relieves

La lluvia, pie danzante y largo pelo,
el tobillo mordido por el rayo,
desciende acompañada de tambores:
abre los ojos el maíz, y crece.

OCTAVIO PAZ
de "En Uxmal"

Reliefs

The rain, dancing, long-haired,
ankles slivered by lightning,
descends, to an accompaniment of drums:
the corn opens its eyes, and grows.

OCTAVIO PAZ
Translated by Muriel Rukeyser
from "In Uxmal"

Prayer to the Corn in the Field

Sacred food
sacred bones

don't go to another house
don't go at all

come straight in to us
stay right on the trail

to the house
to your bed

don't go crying like an orphan
to another plant

another stone
another cave

kernels that fall out of you
that I didn't find to pick up

if there are those of you
who were taken from your places

by the mountain lion
by the squirrel

by the coyote
by the fox

by the pig
by the thief

come back along the trail
to our house

the whole time
to our place

don't get smaller
going away

from our feet
from our hands

Mayan poem related by Am Pérez Mesa (Tenejapa)
Literal version from Tzeltal into Spanish
by Katherine B. Branstetter
Translated by W. S. Merwin

The Toad and a Buzzard

What is written here are very old words, because it used to be that animals talked.

There was a toad and buzzard. Toads used to walk about like dogs. They didn't know how to hop.

Well, the toad was standing on top of a rock. When it saw a buzzard flying above, it called out, "Uncle John! Uncle John?"

Although the toad was shouting, Uncle John had a hard time hearing it. But when the buzzard understood his nephew's words, he glided quickly down to the ground.

"What do you want, Nephew, that you are shouting so?" asked the buzzard.

"I want to ask you if it is true that there are fiestas in the sky," said the toad.

"Yes, indeed, there are wonderful fiestas there."

"Can you carry me up? I want to see the fiestas!"

"Fine," the buzzard said. "Let's go, climb on top of me."

Well, the toad just rose up. They were soaring. When they were halfway there, the awful toad asked, "Uncle, why does your head stink so much?"

"That's the way we always are," said the buzzard. He added, "Don't say that to me again, or I'll throw you off."

Well, they traveled another stretch, and the toad spoke. "Ah, Uncle, why does your head smell so bad to me?"

"Be quiet, please. It's the second time you said that to me. If you mention it three times, I'll drop you down."

"I won't say it again because I really want to see the fiesta."

They were almost there.

But the toad cried out, "Uncle! I think your head smells really rotten!"

"Forgive me, Nephew, I'm going to toss you down," said the buzzard.

The toad landed—smash!—on the ground. Its legs were terribly squashed. Now it couldn't stand up. That's the way it was left. And that's why the toad walks about with hops. That's why the toad never arrived at the fiesta, because of what it said to its uncle, the buzzard.

REYMUNTO KOMES ERNANTES
Translated from the Tzotzil by Robert M. Laughlin

La tortuga

Aunque jamás se muda,
a tumbos, como carro de mudanzas,
va por la senda la tortuga.

JOSÉ JUAN TABLADA
de "Haiku de un día"

The Turtle

Although he never leaves home,
the turtle, like a load of furniture,
lurches down the path.

JOSÉ JUAN TABLADA
Translated by Judith Infante
from "Haiku of a Day"

La vida (Life), José Jesús Chán Guzmán

El fuego y el tlacuache

Dicen que esta era una vieja que consiguió detener la lumbre cuando apenas se desprendió de algunas estrellas o planetas. Ella no tuvo miedo y fue a traerla donde se cayó la lumbre y así la detuvo mucho tiempo, hasta que llegó un tiempo en que todos pensaron que esa lumbre iba a ser para todos y no para la vieja nada más y entonces se iban las gentes a la casa de la vieja a pedir lumbre; pero la vieja se puso brava y no quería dar a ninguno. Entonces intervino el Tlacuache y dijo a los asistentes:

—Yo, Tlacuache, me comprometo a regalar la lumbre, si no me van a comer ustedes. Entonces, hubo una burla muy grande al pobre animal, pero éste, muy sereno, contestó así:

—No me sigan burlando, porque la burla es para ustedes mismos, no es para mí, así que esta misma tarde verán ustedes cumplidas mis promesas.

Al caer la tarde del mismo día, pasó el Tlacuache visitando casa por casa diciendo que él iba a traer la lumbre hasta donde está la vieja, pero que los demás recogieran cuanto puedan. Y así llegó hasta la casa de la vieja y le habló así:

—Buenas tardes, Señora Lumbre, ¡qué frío hace! Yo quisiera estar un rato junto a la lumbre y calentarme, porque me muero de frío.

La vieja creyó que era cierto que tenía frío el Tlacuache y le admitió acercarse a la lumbre el Tlacuache; pero éste, muy astuto se fue arrimando más y más hasta poder meterse en la lumbre, metiendo su cola y así poder llevar. Pues una vez ardiendo su cola se fue corriendo a repartir la lumbre hasta donde pudo alcanzar.

Y fue por eso que hasta ahora los tlacuaches tienen la cola pelada.

CARLOS INCHÁUSTEGUI

Fire and the Opossum

It is told that long ago there was an old woman who succeeded in capturing fire when it first broke loose from the stars and planets. She was not afraid, and went to the place where it fell to gather it, and she kept it for a long while. But there came a time when the others thought that the fire should be for everyone and not only for the old woman, so they came to her house to ask for some.

The old lady got very mad and would not give away any of her fire. A long time passed and word got around that the old woman was keeping the fire and did not want to share it. Then the Opossum stepped up and said to the gathering, "I, Tlacuache, will undertake to get and give away fire if you will promise never to eat me again."

Then everyone made fun of the poor Opossum. He, keeping cool, answered, "Stop scoffing! The scoffs will turn back on you. They are not for me. By this evening you will see that I have kept my promise."

That same afternoon the Opossum visited every house, saying that he would get the fire from the place where the old woman lived, but when he came back to deliver it to them, they must be ready. And in this manner, he reached the old woman's house and said, "Good afternoon, Madame Fire! How cold it is! I would like your permission to stay by your fire for warmth, because I'm freezing!"

The old woman believed the Opossum was cold and allowed him to come close to the fire. Very slyly, he crept closer and closer until he was nearly on top of it, and then he put his tail right into it so he could carry some away! As soon as his tail caught fire he ran from there and distributed the fire to as many homes as he could.

And that is why, even today, all Opossums have a hairless, naked tail.

CARLOS INCHÁUSTEGUI
Translated by Consuelo de Aerenlund

75

Cruzando la linea (Crossing the Line), Teresa Zimbrón

La mosca

1

Porque la mosca es sucia
y despreciable,
pero tan familiar
como el cochambre de la estufa,
como la bacinica del abuelo,
como el salitre de las paredes,
como una mancha oscura
en el mantel,
como un bolillo húmedo,
como el olor del gato,
como los calcetines
en remojo;
porque la mosca vuela hipnotizada
en la sala vacía,
junto al balcón abierto,
cuando la tarde presagia lluvia,
su presencia nos punza
y nos contenta
Ella es el ángel nuestro
de las alas turbias,
un recado confuso
que nos une a la vida

2

Dulce animal casero,
fantasma tolerable:
no engordes demasiado,
no insistes en chocar
contra los focos,
no fastidies al perro,
no roces nuestros labios,
no te seques en una telaraña,
no recorras los bordes
de las cazuelas sucias,
pero ante todo
no caigas en la sopa
—y no faltes en casa
ni de noche ni de día

EDUARDO HURTADO

The Fly

1

Because the fly is filthy
and despicable,
but so homely
like the grime on the stove,
like Grandfather's chamber pot,
like the dampness on the walls,
like a dark stain
on the tablecloth,
like a soggy roll,
like the smell of the cat,
like socks
left to soak;
because the fly buzzes hypnotized
in the empty living room,
by the open balcony,
when the afternoon suggests rain,
its presence pricks us
and makes us content
It is our angel
of blurred wings,
a confused message
that unites us with life

2

Dear house pet,
tolerable phantom:
don't get too fat,
don't insist on crashing
into the light bulbs,
don't pester the dog,
don't graze our lips,
don't shrivel up in a spider's web,
don't circle the rims
of the dirty pots
but above all
don't fall in the soup
—and be sure to be home
both night and day

EDUARDO HURTADO
Translated by C. M. Mayo

El grillo

La noche tiene su brillo,
su música y su silencio...
pues cada estrella es un grillo
entre la hierba del cielo.

La hormiga

En esta tierra el viajero
no ha de sentarse un minuto
porque un volcán diminuto
¡puede ser un hormiguero!

La polilla

Limpias la mesa y las sillas
las camas y los sillones;
mas si limpias los cajones
¿qué comerán las polillas?

La catarina

La catarina de lejos
me recuerda ciertos rostros
con los lunares muy negros
y con los labios muy rojos.

La luciérnaga

En el campo el corazón
y la luna son hermanos;
y las luciérnagas son
estrellitas en las manos.

La abeja

Cuando te vas a acostar
una abeja puedes ser:
tu cama es como un panal
y tus sueños son la miel.

ALBERTO BLANCO
de "También los insectos son perfectos"

The Cricket

The night contains his wit,
his music and his silence,
for each star is a cricket
in the grass of the sky.

The Ant

In this country a traveler
cannot sit for a minute
because a miniature volcano
turns out to be an anthill!

The Moth

Clear off the table and the chairs
the beds and the sofas;
but if you clean out the drawers
what will the moths eat?

The Ladybug

From the distance the ladybug
reminds me of certain faces
with dark black moles
and bright red lips.

The Firefly

In the country, heart
and moon are brothers,
and in your hands
the fireflies are little stars.

The Honey Bee

When you go to bed
you can be a bee:
your bed is like the honey comb
and your dreams the honey.

ALBERTO BLANCO
Translated by Judith Infante
from "Insects Are Perfect Too"

Golondrina

El primer día voló sobre el kiosco
(Un vuelo de reconocimiento)
Del segundo al sexto construyó el nido
(A castillos en el aire, andamios de plumas)
El séptimo descansó viendo llegar a
   las demás
(Eran cientos, miles)

EDUARDO MARTÍNEZ

The Swallow

The first day he flew over the shed
(He was surveying it)

From the second to sixth he built the nest
(To castles in the air, scaffolds of feathers)

The seventh he rested, watching the
   others arrive
(They were hundreds, thousands)

EDUARDO MARTÍNEZ
Translated by Judith Infante

A un pajarillo

Canoro:
te alejas
de rejas
de oro.

Y al coro
le dejas
las quejas
y el lloro.

Que vibre
ya libre
tu acento.

Las alas
son galas
del viento.

CELEDONIO JUNCO DE LA VEGA

To a Little Bird

Melodious:
you keep your distance
from golden bars.

And to song
you leave your
complaints
and wails.

Let your voice
vibrate
freely.

Wings
are the wind's
festivities.

CELEDONIO JUNCO DE LA VEGA
Translated by Joan Darby Norris

El coyote y el conejo (The Coyote and the Rabbit), Gerardo Suzan

Las orejas del conejo

Una vez, hace miles de años, el conejo tenía las orejas muy pequeñas, tan pequeñas como las orejas de un gatito. El conejo estaba contento con sus orejas, pero no con el tamaño de su cuerpo. Él quería ser grande, tan grande como el lobo o el coyote o el león.

Un día cuando iba saltando por los campos, el conejo vio al león, rey de los animales, cerca del bosque.

—¡Qué grande y hermoso es!— dijo el conejo. —Y yo soy tan pequeño y feo.

El conejo estaba tan triste que se sentó debajo de un árbol y comenzó a llorar amargamente.

—¿Qué tienes, conejito? ¿Por qué lloras?— preguntó la lechuza que vivía en el árbol.

—Lloro porque quiero ser grande, muy grande— dijo el conejito.

La lechuza era un pájaro sabio. Cerró los ojos por dos o tres minutos para pensar en el problema y luego dijo:

—Conejito, debes visitar al dios de los animales. Creo que él puede hacerte más grande.

—Mil gracias, lechuza sabia. Voy a visitarlo ahora— respondió el conejo. Y fue saltando a la colina donde vivía el dios.

—Buenos días. ¿Cómo estás?— dijo el dios de los animales cuando vio al conejito.

—Buenos días, señor. Estoy triste porque soy tan pequeño. Su majestad, ¿podría hacerme grande, muy grande?

—¿Por qué quieres ser grande?— preguntó el dios con una sonrisa.

—Si soy grande, algún día puedo ser el rey de los animales en vez del león.

—Muy bien, pero primero tienes que hacer tres cosas difíciles. Entonces voy a decidir si debo hacerte más grande o no.

—¿Qué tengo que hacer?

—Mañana tienes que traerme la piel de un lagarto, de un mono y de una culebra.

—Muy bien, señor. Hasta mañana.

El conejo estaba alegre. Fue saltando, saltando al río. Aquí vio a su amigo, el lagarto pequeño.

—Amigo lagarto, ¿podrías prestarme tu piel elegante hasta mañana? La necesito para…

—Para una fiesta, ¿no?— dijo el lagarto antes de que el conejo pudiera decir la verdad.

—Sí, sí— respondió rápidamente el conejo.

—¡Ay, qué gran honor para mí! Aquí la tienes.

Con la piel del lagarto, el conejo visitó al mono y a la culebra. Cada amigo le dio al conejo su piel para la fiesta.

Muy temprano a la mañana siguiente, el conejo fue despacio, muy despacio, con las pieles pesadas ante el dios de los animales.

—Aquí estoy con las pieles— gritó felizmente el conejo pequeño.

El dios estaba sorprendido. Pensó: "¡Qué astuto es este conejito!" Pero en voz alta dijo:

—Si te hago más grande, puede ser que hagas daño a los otros animales sin quererlo. Por eso voy a hacer grandes solamente tus orejas. Así puedes oír mejor y eso es muy útil cuando tus enemigos estén cerca.

El dios tocó las orejas pequeñas del conejo y como por arte de magia, se le hicieron más grandes. El conejo no tuvo tiempo de decir nada, ni una palabra.

—Mil gracias, buen dios. Usted es sabio y amable. Ahora estoy muy feliz— dijo el conejo. Y fue saltando, saltando por los campos con las pieles que devolvió a sus amigos con gratitud.

Y desde aquel día el conejo vivió muy contento con su cuerpo pequeño y sus orejas grandes.

DE ORIGEN MAYA

The Rabbit's Ears

Long, long ago there was a time when Rabbit looked very much the way he looks now, except for his ears. Rabbit's ears were about as small as a cat's ears. He was content with his ears, but he was unhappy about the size of his body. He wanted to be large, as large as Wolf, Coyote, or even Lion.

One day when Rabbit was hopping in the field near the forest, he saw Lion, King of the Animals. "Lion is so great and beautiful," sighed Rabbit. "And I am so little and ugly." Feeling sad, Rabbit sat under a tree and cried bitter tears.

"Rabbit, why are you crying?" asked Owl from his tree.

"I'm crying because I want to be large, very large," said Rabbit.

Owl, being very wise, closed his eyes for two or three minutes and thought seriously about Rabbit's problem, then said, "Little Rabbit, you ought to visit the God of the Animals. Only he can make you large."

"A thousand thanks, Wise Owl. I am going to visit him now," answered Rabbit.

Rabbit quickly hopped up the hill where the God of the Animals lived.

"Good day, Little Rabbit. How are you?" asked the God of the Animals when he saw him.

"Good day, Señor. I am sad because I am so small. Your Majesty, could you make me large? Very large?"

"Why do you want to be large?" asked the God of the Animals, smiling.

"If I were large," said Rabbit, "one day I might be able to become king of the animals instead of Lion."

"Very well," said the God of the Animals. "But first you must do three difficult things before I decide if I should make you larger or not."

"What do I need to do?"

"Tomorrow, bring me the skins of Alligator, Monkey, and Snake."

"Very well, Señor. Until tomorrow!"

Rabbit was happy! He went hopping off to the river to find his friend, Alligator.

"Friend Alligator, could you lend me your elegant skin until tomorrow? I need it for…"

"For a fiesta, right?" interrupted Alligator.

"Yes, yes, for a fiesta," answered Rabbit quickly.

"Oh, what a great honor for me! Here it is."

With the skin of Alligator, Rabbit visited Monkey and Snake. Each friend willingly gave Rabbit his skin for the fiesta.

Early the next morning, Rabbit slowly, very slowly, dragged the heavy skins before the God of the Animals. "Here I am with the skins!" the small Rabbit yelled happily.

The God of the Animals was quite surprised.

"What a clever Rabbit!" he thought. Then the God told Rabbit of his decision. "Rabbit, I am concerned that if I make you much larger, it is possible that the other animals may be hurt by you. Therefore, I will only make your ears large. Very large. This will help you hear better and will be more useful to you when your enemies are near."

Before Rabbit could say a word, the God touched Rabbit's small ears and instantly they became larger. "A thousand thanks. You are so wise and kind. I am very happy," said Rabbit. He left, hopping, hopping toward the field to return the skins to his friends.

And since that day Rabbit has lived contentedly with his small body and large ears.

A MAYAN STORY
Translated by Mary Guerrero Milligan

de Carta explicándole a la niña Paola
el vuelo del colibrí

Cuando el colibrí se posa
ojos de papel volando
anda loca de amor
la chuparrosa...

DANTE MEDINA

from Letter Explaining the
Hummingbird's Flight to Little Paola

When the hummingbird alights
paper eyes flying
it goes crazy with love
the rose sipper...

DANTE MEDINA
Translated by Joan Darby Norris and Barry Norris

Los pájaros

   Pájaros,
que son el mismo cielo,
y se liberan de Dios,
y vuelan.

Pájaros picoteando el agua.

RAMIRO LOMELÍ

Birds

   Birds,
they are heaven itself,
and get free from God,
and fly.

Birds pecking the water.

RAMIRO LOMELÍ
Translated by Raúl Aceves and Alejandro Vargas

de *Refranes*

No hay pájaro que viva triste
si tiene corazón, canción y alpiste.

MARGARITA ROBLEDA MOGUEL

from *Proverbs*

No bird alive can be sad
if it has a heart, a song, and seed.

MARGARITA ROBLEDA MOGUEL
Translated by Mary Guerrero Milligan

Reflexiones (Reflections), Kathleen Clement

Agua y tierra

El agua
es la luz
con raíz en la tierra.

Beberla
es echarse a caminar
   como un río.

RAÚL BAÑUELOS

Water and Earth

Water
is the light
with roots on earth.

To drink it
is to journey
like a river.

RAÚL BAÑUELOS
Translated by Yvette Grutter and Joan Darby Norris

Devolver el agua

Un recuerdo es tanto
y nada:
un balneario
me visita con su larga capa de agua,
su máscara azul,
su brillo de ojos transparentes,
su gente brotando
en un charco de cielo.

Es todo y poco:
con la miel en su espalda
y una colmena de manos,
la muchacha le muestra la luna al sol.

LUIS MEDINA GUTIÉRREZ

Return the Water

A memory is so much
and nothing:
a swimming pool
visits me with its long water cape,
its blue mascara,
the shine of its transparent eyes,
its people blossoming
in a puddle of sky.

It is everything and so little:
with the honey on her shoulders
and beehive hands,
the girl shows the moon to
the sun.

LUIS MEDINA GUTIÉRREZ
Translated by Joan Darby Norris

Tritón

La lluvia
nada libremente,
curvea su lomo de rayas.
Estirándose
como gato amodorrado,
se va por
el ombligo del patio.

LUIS MEDINA GUTIÉRREZ

Triton*

The rain
swims freely,
curving its striped loins.
Stretching itself
like a drowsy cat,
it heads for
the navel of the patio.

LUIS MEDINA GUTIÉRREZ
Translated by Joan Darby Norris

Hermano Sol

Hermano Sol, cuando te plazca, vamos
a colocar la tarde donde quieras.
Tiene la milpa edad para que hicieras
con puñados de luz sonoros tramos.

Si en la última piedra nos sentamos
verás cómo caminan las hileras
y las hormigas de tu luz raseras
moverán prodigiosos miligramos.

Se fue haciendo la tarde con las flores
silvestres. Y unos cuantos resplandores
sacaron de la luz el tiempo oscuro.

Que acomodó el silencio; con las manos
encendimos la estrella y como hermanos
caminamos detrás de un hondo muro.

CARLOS PELLICER

Brother Sun

Brother Sun, when it pleases you we will go
to hang the afternoon wherever you want.
The cornfield is old enough for you to make
sound waves with fistfuls of light.

If we sit down on the last rock
you will see how the rows march
and the little ants in your light
will move wondrous milligrams.

You've turned the wildflowers into the
afternoon. And a few radiant beams
have taken the darkness from within the day.

You brought the silence; by hand,
we light the stars and like brothers
walk behind a deep wall.

CARLOS PELLICER
Translated by Joan Darby Norris

*Triton—a god of the sea, son of Poseidon

Carta recordando el perro que tuvo Agnés

Era un perro candor,
trafica corazón, trafica niños.
A la hora del ya-no
        (A la hora-niña),
vino a saltar amor con buenos días.
Vaya con un no-ver
        perro de puros ojos: puro perro,
que salga lo carajo, entre lo niña,
perro que te andas perro con el día;
¿a quién le haces las cosas?
        (palabras que nos barren,
        qué perro, qué decías, algo
        que no escribí, qué pues que
        con la rima, ah sí:)
úpale: ¡le acabas de inventar seis pies a la
        alegría!

DANTE MEDINA

Letter Remembering the Dog That Agnes Once Had

He was a simple dog,
heart dealer, child dealer.
At the time of "that's enough"
        (at the little girl-time)
he came leaping love with good morning.
Go without seeing
        dog of all eyes: all dog,
let that anger out of the child,
dog, you're just a dog all day;
for whom do you do things?
        (words that sweep us,
        what a dog, what were you saying,
        something that I didn't write,
        what about with rhyme, oh yes:)
oops: you've just added six feet to happiness!

DANTE MEDINA
Translated by Joan Darby Norris and Barry Norris

Angel azul (Blue Angel), Rodolfo Morales

Los perros peregrinos

—¡Pelón, pelonete, cabeza de cohete!

Así gritaba Ignacia, cuando veía a aquel perrito tan cómico para ella, pues carecía de pelo.

Era de los pocos perros xolozcuintli que todavía se podían ver en su pueblo enclavado en la sierra de Guerrero. Y más extraño era el hecho de que "Pelonete", como lo llamaba la niña, era un callejero empedernido. Así lo había sido desde que había escapado de la casa de un señor muy rico, dueño de un criadero donde se encontraban varios de sus hermanitos. Ese hombre criaba a los perros de raza azteca para venderlos a precios muy altos en Europa y en Estados Unidos.

Aquella tarde, Ignacia vio a Pelonete en su parcela comiendo un elote en el maizal. Se acercó despacio y le dijo suavemente en "mexicano" (náhuatl):

—Chichitu (perrito), ¡Amo uaualoa! (¡No ladres!)

Ignacia hablaba español y mexicano, pero para hablar con Pelonete decidió usar este último idioma.

—¿Tlacuas ti nequi? (¿Quieres comer?) ¡Niauh ompa mo chan! (¡Vamos a mi casa!) Y se lo llevó abrazado, envuelto en su rebozo.

Al llegar a su casa tuvo que esconderlo bajo el lavadero, para que su mamá no lo descubriera.

Apenas salió al mercado su madre, ella quiso mostrarle la casa a Pelonete. Lo primero que le enseñó fue el vistoso nacimiento, indicio de que la Nochebuena estaba cerca.

El perro pelón miró con entusiasmo las figuras de barro de los Reyes Magos, la Virgen y San José, el lugar cubierto de heno reservado para el niño Dios y, junto, un buey y un burro.

"¿Campa ca in itzcuintli?" (¿Dónde está el perro?)— pensó y siguió mirando.

Lo que más le sorprendió fue el camello, a quien llamó "Tepotzolli" o "jorobado".

Entonces se le soltó la lengua y, para sorpresa de Ignacia, comenzó a hablar y a partir de ahí, ¿quién podía pararlo?

—En la época de mis antepasados —decía— ya se comían algunas de las cosas que tienen preparadas para su cena de esta noche, como el guajolote. ¡Ah! y además, las frutas que contiene esa ensalada las comían mis abuelos perros y sus amos. También esas otras con las que van a llenar aquella olla.

—¿Cocómo cucuáles?— dijo Ignacia, aún algo asustada.

—Las jícamas, los tejocotes, los cacahuates, los zapotes…

—¿Zapotes? ¡Ay, la traviesa de mi hermana María le quiere poner zapotes a la piñata! ¡Ji, jiii! ¿Te imaginas, Pelonete, las manos y las caras de los niños llenos de zapote? —dijo la niña, abrazando al perro para sentir su piel, más calientita que la de otros perros.

—¡Sí, guau guau! —dijo Pelonete—. Lo que también me parece familiar es una flor roja de hojas laargas, laargas…

—Es la Flor de Nochebuena…

Ignacia y Pelonete no pudieron seguir platicando. Se escuchaba en el patio de la casa el jolgorio de chiquillos. Eran los amiguitos de Nacha que venían a pedir posada.

—Eeen el nombre del cielooooooooo… —cantaban—. Yo oos pido posaaaaaadaaa… En la noche cubierta de estrellas sus velitas brillaban y centellaban.

La familia de Ignacia llegó en ese momento y recibió a los peregrinos con sus buñuelos y atole, que los chiquillos comieron con gran alborozo.

Horas después, al irse todos los niños, la familia se quedó sola para compartir la cena de Navidad.

—Esta noche es Nochebuena, Nochebuena, y mañana es Navidad —cantaron los hermanitos de Ignacia.

Ante el asombro de nuestra amiga, su mamá, lejos de enojarse con ella por haber recogido al perro callejero, lo recibió con gusto e incluso le dio de comer carne y tortillas.

Pelonete, después de devorar esos manjares, que para él eran la cena navideña, se quedó ensimismado contemplando el nacimiento.

Ignacia y su familia festejaban tan alegremente, que no se dieron cuenta de que algo extraordinario había pasado.

Pelonete sí lo notó y fue para él la mayor satisfacción de la noche.

Al lado del pesebre, en donde a las 12 de la noche en punto habían colocado al niño Dios, se encontraban nuevas figuras de barro aparecidas como por arte de magia. ¡Eran perros! ¡Y tantos como razas existen! El itzcuintli Pelonete pudo distinguir entre otros, un Alaskan Malamut, un pastor alemán y un Poodle francés.

Todos ladraban de gusto ante el Niño. Este agradecía con su manita las muestras de cariño de todos los perros del mundo, que habían llegado a visitarlo esa noche, como perros peregrinos.

QUETZALCOATL VIZUEL

The Pilgrim Dogs

"Hairless, baldy, firecracker head!" That's what Ignacia screamed when she saw that dog who had no hair and looked so funny to her.

He was one of the few *xolozcuintli*** dogs that still lived in her town, tucked away in the mountains of Guerrero. Even stranger was the fact that "Baldy," as she called him, was a hardened street dog. That's how he had lived ever since he had escaped from the home of a very rich man, a breeder, who was still in possession of many of his brothers and sisters. The man bred these Aztec dogs to sell them for very high prices in Europe and the United States.

That afternoon, Ignacia saw Baldy on her land eating an ear of corn in the cornfield. She approached him slowly and spoke to him gently in Náhuatl. *"Chichitu* (little dog), *amo uaualoa!* (Don't bark!)."

Ignacia spoke Spanish and Náhuatl****, but to speak with Baldy she used her native language.

"Tlacuas ti nequi?" (Do you want to eat?) *"Niauh ompa mo chan!"* (Let's go to my house!) And she carried him in her arms, wrapped up in her shawl.

When she arrived at her house, she hid him under the outdoor sink so that her mother wouldn't notice him.

As soon as her mother left for the market, she gave Baldy a tour of her house.

The first thing she showed him was the colorful manger scene, evidence that Christmas was coming soon.

The hairless dog looked happily at the clay figures of the three wise men, Mary and Joseph, the straw filled manger waiting for the baby Jesus and, standing together, an ox and a burro.

---

*xolozcuintli—hairless breed of Mexican dog dating from pre-Columbian times
**Náhuatl—the Uto-Axtecan language of the Náhuati people in southern Mexico and Central America

"Campa ca in itzcuintli?" (Where is the dog?) he thought, and continued to stare at the figures. The most amazing was the camel, called *"Tepotzolli"* or "hunchback."

At that moment his tongue was set free and, much to the surprise of Ignacia, he began to talk and from then on no one could stop him.

"In the time of my ancestors," he said, "they used to eat some of the foods you have prepared for your Christmas Eve dinner such as turkey. Ah, and not only that, the fruits of that luscious salad were eaten by my dog grandparents and their masters. Also those other things there that are used to stuff into the big empty pot for the piñata."

"Li-like wh-what?" asked Ignacia, still somewhat frightened.

"The *jicamas**, the hawthorn fruits, the peanuts, the *zapotes***..."

"*Zapotes?* Ay, my naughty sister María wants to put *zapotes* in the piñata! Can you imagine, Baldy, the children's hands and faces full of gooey *zapote?*" said the girl, hugging the little dog to feel his skin, which is warmer than that of other dogs.

"Yes, bowwow!" said Baldy. "That red flower also looks familiar to me, the one with the looong, looong red leaves..."

"It's a poinsettia..."

Ignacia and Pelonete couldn't continue their discussion. They heard the boisterous sounds of little children coming from the patio. They were Ignacia's friends who had come to ask for shelter in the traditional reenactment of Joseph and Mary's search for lodging on Christmas Eve.

"In the name of heaven...," they sang. "I ask you for shelter for my wife Mary...." In the star-filled night, their candles twinkled and glowed.

Ignacia's family arrived at that moment to greet the singing pilgrims with *buñuelos* (doughnuts) and *atole* (a thick corn drink), which the little ones ate and drank with delight.

Hours later, after everyone had left, the family sat down to enjoy their own Christmas Eve supper.

"Tonight is Christmas Eve, Christmas Eve, and tomorrow is Christmas," sang the brothers and sisters of Ignacia.

Although our friend had been worried, her mother was far from being angry about the street dog. She welcomed him and gave him meat and tortillas to eat.

Baldy, after devouring his food, which was his Christmas dinner, continued to daydream about the nativity scene.

Ignacia and her family were having such a good time, they failed to notice that something extraordinary had happened.

Baldy did notice, and for him it was the greatest delight of the evening.

On one side of the manger, where exactly at midnight they had placed the baby Jesus, they found that new clay figures had appeared as if by magic. They were dogs! As many different breeds as there are! Baldy saw among others an Alaskan malamute, a German shepherd, and a French poodle.

All barked with pleasure for the baby Jesus. With his little hands raised he received the love of all the dogs of the world, who as pilgrims, had arrived to visit him that night.

QUETZALCOATL VIZUEL
Translated by Joan Darby Norris

*jicamas—a tropical plant with an edible root that resembles a giant, pale rutabaga and tastes slightly sweet
**zapotes—the sweet plum-like fruit of the marmalade tree

Turasnuun

Vu'une turasnuun
ti vo'nee ch'inun to'ox
ta to'ox slo'bun kanal
ti chijetike, batz'i vokol li ch'i tajmek
yu'un ja' li' chtal to'ox
tajmek sk'el ti schijike,
tana li'e ilbaj xiyutik
ti keremotike,
ta sbasolanik ti koke ti jk'obtake
ta slilinik ti jnichtake.
pere ti k'alal chkak' ti
jsate mu xa smalaik ora
chta'aj une', tze no'ox
ta slo'bikun.
Ja' jech li'e
il baj xi yutikun
ja' ti jtuk tuk li'
ch'iemune, naka yantik o ti jchi'iltak
li' ta jxokone, xchi'uk k'alal tzotz
chtal ti ik'e
mu xak' satin kun.
yu'un ta slilin lok'el
ti jnichtake, ti
kuni satake
ja' no'ox chiyich' ta
k'ux ti vo'ch'ich'i oe.

PANCHO ERNANTES ERNANTES
Original Tzotzil version

I Am a Peach Tree

I am a peach tree.
I used to be little.
The sheep used to eat my leaves.
I had a very hard time growing up
because the sheep would come so
    often to see me.

Now the boys bother me,
they keep cutting my trunk and my branches.
They shake down my flowers.
When I produce fruits,
they don't wait for them to ripen,
They just eat them green.
That's how they bother me.

Since I grew up alone,
all my companions around me seem different.
When the wind blows hard,
my flowers and little fruits are blown away.

But the rain cares for me, so I will grow.

PANCHO ERNANTES ERNANTES
Translated from the Tzotzil by Robert M. Laughlin

Última etapa (Last Stage), Mario Rangel

Valle de bravo (Brave Valley), Kathleen Clement

de *Estrofas en la playa*

El río viene de secretas grutas,
desconocidas fuentes.
A mirarlo pasar corren los árboles,
adiós le dicen los follajes verdes.

Para que el cielo sepa qué caminos
llevan al mar, para que aprenda el campo
una nueva canción y el día tenga
dónde mojar los pies,
el río viene izando su largo nombre líquido.
Ay, del que junto al río
no quiere llamarse sed.

ROSARIO CASTELLANOS

from Verses at the Shore

The river flows from secret caverns,
and undiscovered springs.
When the trees see the river pass, they run too,
calling good-bye with their green leaves…

So that the sky knows which roads
    lead to the sea,
so that the fields learn a new song
and the day has a place to wet its feet,
the river raises its long liquid name.
Oh, whoever stays by a river
won't ever know about thirst.

ROSARIO CASTELLANOS
Translated by Judith Infante

Derecho de propiedad

¡Nada es tan mío
como el mar
cuando lo miro!

ELÍAS NANDINO

Property Rights

Nothing is more mine
than the sea
when I look at it!

ELÍAS NANDINO
Translated by Judith Infante

Nunca podré conocer el mar

Nunca podré conocer el mar
siempre que viene
   se va

ERIKA RAMÍREZ DIEZ

I Will Never Be Able to Know the Sea

I will never be able to know the sea
Every time it arrives
   it leaves

ERIKA RAMÍREZ DIEZ
Translated by Joan Darby Norris

La enredadera

Recostado en la hierba del jardín,
me llamó la atención la enredadera.
Levanté con las manos la cabeza
para mirar su impulso de raíz.
Y supe que en su fuga se concentran
los ritmos de las sombras y un fluir
de insectos en las hojas. Comprendí
por ella la salud de la sorpresa.
Incorporé la espalda ante el prodigio
de la verde cortina vegetal.
Me sacudió su exuberancia en orden.
Y entendí su silencio primitivo,
su terca lentitud, su oscuridad,
sus notas graves y su fuga enorme.

VÍCTOR MANUEL MENDIOLA

The Climbing Vine

As I lay down in the garden grass,
the climbing vine came to my attention.
With my hands I lifted my head
to look at its impulse of roots.
And I knew that in its escape are concentrated
the rhythms of shadows and a flow
of insects in the leaves. I understood
because of it the blessing of a surprise.
I sat up before the wonder
of the green floral curtain.
I was shaken by its exuberant order.
And I understood its primitive silence,
its stubborn slowness, its darkness,
its grave notes and its enormous flight.

VÍCTOR MANUEL MENDIOLA
Translated by Jennifer Clement

Niño con paloma (*Child with Dove*), José Jesús Chán Guzmán

El llanto

Al declinar la tarde, se acercan los amigos;
pero la vocecita no deja de llorar.
Cerramos las ventanas, las puertas, los postigos,
pero sigue cayendo la gota de pesar.

No sabemos de dónde viene la vocecita;
registramos la granja, el establo, el pajar.
El campo en la tibieza del blando sol dormita,
pero la vocecita no deja de llorar.

—¡La noria que chirría! —dicen los más
   agudos—
Pero ¡si aquí no hay norias! ¡Qué cosa singular!
Se contemplan atónitos, se van quedando
   mudos,
porque la vocecita no deja de llorar.

Ya es franca desazón lo que antes era risa
y se adueña de todos un vago malestar,
y todos se despiden y se escapan de prisa,
porque la vocecita no deja de llorar.

Cuando llega la noche, ya el cielo es un sollozo
y hasta finge un sollozo la leña del hogar.
A solas, sin hablarnos, lloramos sin embozo,
pero la vocecita no deja de llorar.

ALFONSO REYES

The Cry

At the closing of the day, the friends gather,
but the little voice doesn't stop crying.
We close the windows, the doors, the shutters,
but the droplets of sorrow continue to fall.

We don't know where the little voice comes
   from;
we check the farm, the stable, the haystack.
The countryside dozes in the coolness of the
   pale sun,
but the little voice doesn't stop crying.

"It must be the pump squeaking!" say the
   sharpest ones.
But there are no pumps here! How strange!
Astonished, they become silent, one by one,
because the little voice doesn't stop crying.

What was amusing has turned frankly irritating
and all feel slightly uneasy.
Everyone says good-bye and leaves in a hurry,
because the little voice doesn't stop crying.

When night comes, the whole heaven is a sob.
Even the firewood on the hearth pretends to
   weep.
All by ourselves, we grieve openly
but the little voice doesn't stop crying.

ALFONSO REYES
Translated by Joan Darby Norris

Sobresalto

¡Qué perfecto
salto mortal
ha echado el sol
hacia
el otro lado del mar!

ELÍAS NANDINO

Somersault

What a perfect
exhausting leap
the sun has made
toward
the other side of the sea!

ELÍAS NANDINO
Translated by Joan Darby Norris

Irás y no volverás

Sitio de aquellos cuentos infantiles
eres la tierra entera
A todas partes
vamos a no volver
Estamos por vez última
en dondequiera

JOSÉ EMILIO PACHECO

And So You Go, Never to Come Back

Land of those childhood stories
you are the whole world
Everywhere
we go never to come back
For the last time we are
wherever we are

JOSÉ EMILIO PACHECO
Translated by George McWhirter

Arrullo

para Ane

Cuando cae la tarde el sol se da vuelta
la noche cobija para que se duerma.

Llega la luna nana
a cantarle canciones de cuna.

Duérmete ya mi niño glotón
las mejillas te arden de tomar el sol.

Muchacha morena la noche desnuda
se pasea sola por la playa bruna.

Gajo a gajo come la luna naranja
se mece en columpio la noche descalza.

LETICIA HERRERA

Lullaby

for Ane

In late afternoon when the sun turns 'round
night will smooth and turn her covers down.

Then along comes the Aunty Moon
singing her cradle tune.

Go to sleep my songbird child
on your cheek the sun still burns.

A dark-haired girl wearing dusk for a gown
strolls alone on a beach of shadow and sound.

She swings from sea to sky and nibbles the light
from a citron moon, the barefoot night.

LETICIA HERRERA
Translated by Judith Infante

Si el gorrión perdiera sus alas

Si el gorrión perdiera sus alas
la casa su techo
y la mesa sus patas

si el águila en la altura
y la mujer en la plaza
de pronto se deshicieran

si la ciudad con sus torres
y el volcán con sus hoyos
cayeran en un pozo

si los caminos
si los gatos si los ojos
perdieran para siempre el camino

si la Tierra se precipitara
en un espacio negro

si no hubiera más cuerpos
si no hubiera más luz

el canto seguiría

HOMERO ARIDJIS

Should the Sparrow Lose Its Wings

Should the sparrow lose its wings
the house its roof
and the table its legs

should the eagle in the skies
and the woman in the market
crumple into bits

should the city with its towers
and the volcano with its craters
fall into a well

should the roads
should the cats should the eyes
lose their way for always

should the Earth launch itself
into a black hole

should there be no more bodies
should there be no more light

the song would still sing

HOMERO ARIDJIS
Translated by Martha Black Jordan

La luna es tuya

—Mira la luna. La luna es tuya, nadie te la puede quitar. La has atado con los besos de tu mano y con la alegre mirada de tu corazón. Sólo es una gota de luz, una palabra hermosa. Luna es la distante, la soñada, tan irreal como el cielo y como los puntos de las estrellas. La tienes en las manos, hijo, y en tu sonrisa se extiende su luz como una mancha de oro, como un beso derramado. Aceite de los ojos, su claridad se posa como un ave. Descansa en las hojas, en el suelo, en tu mejilla, en las paredes blancas y se acurruca al pie de los árboles como un fantasma fatigado. Leche de luna, ungüento de luna tienen las cosas, y su rostro velado sonríe.

Te la regalo, como te regalo mi corazón y mis días. Te la regalo para que la tires.

JAIME SABINES

The Moon Is Yours

Look at the moon. The moon is yours, no one can take it away from you. You have drawn it to yourself with kisses blown from your hand and the joyful gaze of your heart. It's just a drop of light, a beautiful word. Moon is the distant dreamed-of thing, as unreal as the sky and the tips of the stars. You have it in your hands, son, and in your smile it spreads its light like a patch of gold, like a lost kiss. Oil of the eyes, its splendor alights like a bird. It rests on the leaves, on the ground, on your cheek, on the white walls, and curled up at the foot of the trees like a tired ghost. Moon milk, moon salve, and your veiled face smiles.

I give it to you, as I give you my heart and my days. I give it to you so that you will let it go.

JAIME SABINES
Translated by Joan Darby Norris and Barry Norris

NOTES ON THE CONTRIBUTORS

ERMILO ABREU GÓMEZ was born in 1894 and died in 1971. From 1947 to 1960, he lived in Washington, D.C., where he was in charge of the Division of Philosophy and Letters for the Pan-American Union. He gave lectures all around the United States and liked to tell about his land, the Yucatán. In one of his books he told about Jacinto Canek, who fought alongside many others for the rights of the Mayan people. He also wrote plays for the Theater of the Bat. One of his children's books is *The Magic Goat*.

RAÚL ACEVES was born in Guadalajara in 1951. One of his books of poems is called *The Harps of Lightning* (1990). He has worked on various anthologies of poetry, including *The Poems of the Hummingbird* (1990) and *Poetry of America* (1991), and is well-known for his "fine sense of humor and sage perception—quite oriental or mystical. He has walked a lot in deep search of our roots" (Guadalupe Morfín).

LUIS MIGUEL AGUILAR was born in 1956 in Quintana Roo, a remote area of southern Mexico bordering Belize and Guatemala. He has edited the magazine *Nexos*.

HOMERO ARIDJIS was born in Michoacán in 1940. His first book of poems published in English translation was called *Blue Spaces* (1974). He has been a visiting professor in many places and served as Mexico's ambassador to Switzerland and to the Netherlands. A member of Mexico's Group of 100, an environmental watchdog and research organization, he is leading an international fight against the killing and eating of whales. He has written, "I dream of seeing the face of the earth/mother of beings and mother of my mother/and the face of heaven/father of air and father of my father."

RAÚL BAÑUELOS was born in Guadalajara in 1954 and lives in a popular quarter of the city called Santa Teresita. He studied literature at the University of Guadalajara, where he works as a researcher and coordinates literary workshops. He has published seven books of poems. One of the most recent is called *House of Oneself* (1993). His work is described as being "full of humanity—a big heart in well-expressed words."

ALBERTO BLANCO was born in 1951 and is a prolific writer of poems and children's books, as well as a musician and illustrator. As a child, he liked to lie under the piano while his mother played it. His father worked in a factory producing pigments and inks, and his first "toy armies" were the little tin caps of the paint tubes. He wrote "Barcos" for a catalog of an exhibition of toys made by Mexican artists. One of his poems is called "There Is No Paradise Without Animals." He is a full-time professor in the Department of Languages and Linguistics at the University of Texas at El Paso. He and his wife, Patricia Revan, a well-known illustrator of Mexican children's books, have two children.

ROSARIO CASTELLANOS (1925–1974) was born in Mexico City but spent her childhood in Comitán, Chiapas, the southernmost state in Mexico. She returned to Mexico City for her university education, and studied in Spain. Her passionate, very personal poems helped her become widely known as a radical feminist. Her short stories and novels urged social justice and decried the exploitation of Indians in Chiapas. The editor of this book has seen Indian women in Chiapas close their eyes and fold their hands over their hearts when mentioning the name of Castellanos, who died of accidental electrocution in Israel.

JOSÉ JESÚS CHÁN GUZMÁN was born in Tabasco in 1954. His works were shown at an exhibition, "De Corazón a Corazón" ("From Heart to Heart"), in Mexico City in 1994. He has taught art to children and has also been involved in efforts to save the Lacandon rain forest in southern Mexico. Two books published by the United Nations on rain forest conservation adapted his designs for their covers.

JENNIFER CLEMENT was born in Mexico City in 1962. She founded the Tramontane (Italian for "the other side of the mountain") Poetry Group in 1985. One of the aims of the group is to form a bridge between Spanish-speaking Mexicans and English-speaking U.S. artists and writers. She has worked for Viking/Penguin Press and Times Books. Her poems and translations have appeared widely, and a recent book of hers is called *El próximo extraño* (*The Next Stranger*). Jennifer Clement has two small children.

KATHLEEN CLEMENT takes slide photographs of anything she finds interesting—patterns, textures, landscapes, magazine clippings—and paints superimposed projections onto her canvas, often creating intricate, multilayered pictures. The artist, who began studying with abstract expressionist Frank Gonzales in 1967, has participated in numerous solo and group exhibitions in both Mexico and the United States.

FELIPE DÁVALOS was born in 1942 and has worked as an award-winning painter and printmaker since 1967, after studying at Mexico's Art and Publicity School, National Institute of Fine Arts, and Academy of Applied Arts. He has participated in individual and group shows in Mexico, Central America, Europe, and the United States. Since the mid-1980s the artist has also worked as a children's book illustrator for publishers in Mexico, the United States, and Germany.

CONSUELO DE AERENLUND was born in 1923 in Guatemala and now lives in Mexico. She has translated the works of some Mexican writers into English, and her own poems have appeared in various journals.

CELEDONIO JUNCO DE LA VEGA was born in Matamoros in 1863 and died in 1948. The editorials he wrote for journals and papers in the 1920s brought him notoriety. He also distinguished himself as an orator. He won a prize, called "The Natural Flower," in the floral games of the Centennial of Independence for his ode "To the City of Monterrey." His poem "Hymn to Hidalgo" won a gold medal. One of his books is called *Memories of the Fiesta*. He also wrote for the theater.

ANTONIO DELTORO was born in Mexico City in 1947. He studied economics and has worked on the magazine *Iztapalapa*. One of his poems, celebrating the day Thursday, says, "You eat it in slices like a tangerine and in the afternoon it tastes like an apple."

ADRIANA DÍAZ ENCISO was born in Guadalajara in 1964. She has a degree in communications science and has worked for radio and magazines. Her first book of poems is called *Sombra Abierta* (*Open Shadow*). She currently lives in Mexico City.

PANCHO ERNANTES ERNANTES and REYMUNTO KOMES ERNANTES wrote their pieces in the Tzotzil language when they were each twelve years old. They live in Chamula, a highland Indian town in Chiapas. They have both participated in a literacy program called CHANOB VUN TA BATZ'I K'OP (The School Where You Learn the Genuine Language) with the anthropologist and translator Robert M. Laughlin.

CARMEN ESQUIVEL was born in San Luis Potosí in 1937. Thirty-one years later, teaching herself, she began to paint. Subsequently she attended the Potosí Institute for Fine Arts. Since 1974, she has participated in numerous exhibitions throughout Mexico.

ENRIQUE FLORES was born in 1963 in Oaxaca, where he still works and lives. His favorite techniques are metal engraving and watercolor painting. His work was first shown in the United States in 1990 in the exhibition "Life, Legends and Dreams—Six Painters from Oaxaca." His work was recently featured in the exhibition "Oaxaca: The Poetry of Color."

ALBERTO FORCADA's magical short poems for children appeared in *Despertar* (*To Wake Up*), illustrated by Hermilio Gómez, in a wonderful series of children's books from CIDCLI, Centro de Información y Desarrollo de la Comunicación y la Literatura Infantiles, from Mexico City.

ILIANA FUENTES R. was born in the Tamaulipas region, just below the southern tip of Texas. She studied psychology before she taught herself to paint. In 1979 she helped commemorate the International Year of the Child by illustrating the book *Naranja dulce, limón partido* (*Sweet Orange, Sliced Lemon*). "In the form and color of her work the motifs of Mexican folk painting find expression. These motifs gush forth through her art like fresh water from the spring of the collective unconscious" (Juan Gorman).

FRANCISCO GABILONDO SOLER was born in Orizaba in 1907. At age seventeen he was a swimming champion, and early on tried his hand at boxing, then at bullfighting. In 1930 he began to work for a radio network and was known as "the Joker of Teclado." Later, as "Cri-Cri, el Grillo Cantor," he became a major figure in the popular culture of Mexico. He wrote over 300 songs for children. These songs, which exalted moral and social values, are said to be "part of the foundation of the twentieth-century Mexican collective soul." Many of the poets in this book grew up listening to the songs he composed and now pass them on to their own children. A film of his life was made in 1976.

JULIO GALÁN was born in Muzquiz, Coahuila, in 1958 and studied architecture from 1978 to 1982. His paintings have been exhibited in galleries and museums in Mexico, the United States, and Europe.

HUGO GARCÍA GONZÁLEZ was born in 1964 in Orizaba, Veracruz. As a child he enjoyed things related to Mexican culture as well as foreign cultures, which led him to study humanities. Later he came to the United States to teach American literature and Spanish as a second language in upstate New York. He now works as a college professor at the Universidad de las Americas.

JOSÉ GOROSTIZA was born in 1901. He worked in the government as an ambassador, as secretary of foreign affairs, and on the National Commission of Nuclear Energy, as well as publishing books of poetry.

LETICIA HERRERA ALVAREZ was born in Michoacán in 1954. She has written and published poetry and literary criticism and has been writing novels for children.

EDUARDO HURTADO was born in Mexico City in 1950. He studied literature and works as an editor. He has published four books of poems.

CARLOS INCHÁUSTEGUI was born in Peru in 1924 but has lived in Mexico since 1949. He received a degree in ethnology from the National School of Anthropology and has done extensive field work for the Instituto Nacional Indigenista, as well as investigation for other agencies. He has published many books and articles of ethnology and mythology.

A. L. JÁUREGUI has written poetry and plays for children and is editor of a well-known collection of Mexican patriotic poems.

MARTHA BLACK JORDAN was born in 1932, raised in Mexico City near Chapultepec Park, and carries only sunny memories of rides on the old merry-go-round and roller skating around the Fuente de las Ranas. She is a founding member of the Tramontane Poetry Group. Her translations and poetry have appeared in various journals, including *Mānoa,* from Hawaii.

RAMIRO LOMELÍ was born in Jalisco in 1965. He studied literature and has participated in numerous literary conferences. One of his recent books of poems is called *La tienda de los milagros* (*The Shop of Miracles*).

JULIA LÓPEZ was born in the state of Guerrero in 1936. Before she taught herself to paint, she worked as a model for artists and wrote children's stories. She has exhibited in galleries and museums throughout Mexico and the United States, including a 1991 exhibit in Los Angeles, California, in which her work *A Tunnel of Colors* was featured. "Her art is an act of faith; magical style transferred to secular form. Dogs and snakes, corn, water, painted in the color of her body: the brown of the earth" (Rafael Coronel).

JULIO LÓPEZ SEGURA was born in Veracruz in 1970. While he attended a program in the plastic arts at the University of

Veracruz, he participated in various collective exhibitions. He decided to leave the university in order to enjoy greater freedom to develop his artistic style.

EDUARDO MARTÍNEZ has published his poems for children in *Costal de Versos y Cuentos* from CONAFE (Consejo Nacional de Fomento Educativo) in Mexico City.

DANTE MEDINA was born in Jalisco in 1954. She has been a teacher and researcher at the Centro de Estudios Literarios at the University of Guadalajara. She also directed a Latin American theater group in France.

LUIS MEDINA GUTIÉRREZ was born in 1962 and lives in Guadalajara. He is a literature professor on the faculty of the University of Guadalajara, has won many national writing prizes, and is also a lifeguard. Many of his poems describe his close relationship with water. His book of poems is called *Pools with Fallen Sky*.

VÍCTOR MANUEL MENDIOLA was born in Mexico City in 1954. He studied economics and has been the codirector of a publishing house. In one of his poems he visits the zoo with his son. Later, "The rains made us return/home. Radios. Reflections. Racket./The day/with a thunder shower became confused" (translated by Jennifer Clement).

RODOLFO MORALES is the most beloved artist of the "Oaxaca school." The artists working in this region, a center for folk art production, often use imagery rich in "magical realism" and native Indian culture, myths, and legends. Born in the village of Ocotlán in 1925, Rodolfo Morales received his bachelor's degree in fine art from the Escuela Nacional de Artes Plasticas in San Carlos. In addition to teaching at the Escuela Nacional Preparatoria in Mexico City for many years, he has exhibited extensively throughout Mexico and, more recently, the United States. He is the subject of a monograph published by the State of Veracruz in 1992, and his collages illustrate a book, *Angel's Kite*, a children's story based on his childhood. He now lives again in Ocotlán, where he has established a village youth foundation, as well as a library, theater, and cultural center in his home.

GUADALUPE MORFÍN OTERO was born in 1953 and lives in Guadalajara. She is studying for a master's degree in contemporary literature at the Centro de Estudios Literarios in Guadalajara and often writes about her three children and feminist issues. One of her books is called *En Espera del Ángel* (*The Hope of the Angel*, 1988). Her writings have been included in numerous newspapers and anthologies, including *This Same Sky* (Simon & Schuster Books for Young Readers), edited by Naomi Shihab Nye in 1992, and have been translated into French as well as English.

MYRIAM MOSCONA was born in Mexico City in 1955 into a Bulgarian-Jewish family that had emigrated to Mexico. She is a journalist as well as a poet and also produces radio programs.

ANGELINA MUÑIZ-HUBERMAN was born in 1936. A writer of poems and short stories, she was honored with the Premio Xavier

Villarrutia (literary award) at the age of fifty. Her book *Enclosed Garden* was translated to English in 1988.

ELÍAS NANDINO was born in Jalisco in 1900 and died in 1993. He studied medicine, became a surgeon in 1930, and cultivated a friendship with a group of writers called "The Contemporaries," who fueled his deep interest in poetry. He became chief of service in the Juarez Hospital, and also worked at the penitentiary and in official and private clinics. He founded and edited the journal *Estaciones* and published many poetry books with such interesting titles as *River of Shadow, Shipwreck of Doubt,* and *Triangle of Silences*.

CHAN KIN NORRIS was born in San Quintin, Chiapas, in 1977 and lived in the Lacandon rain forest, speaking Maya until the age of five. He then moved to San Cristobal de Las Casas, where he attended school and liked to draw airplanes. He painted *Moon and Sun Together* while in elementary school. Still a citizen of Mexico, he attends high school in Taos, New Mexico.

FERNANDO OLIVERA's work often focuses on the political struggles in the city of Juchitán. Born in Oaxaca in 1962, he later studied lithography under the Japanese printmaker Zinzaburu Takeda. His work has been exhibited in Mexico City, El Salvador, and the United States. Fernando Olivera is also the illustrator of *The Woman Who Outshone the Sun,* a children's book based on a Mixtec folktale.

JOSÉ EMILIO PACHECO was born in 1939 and spent a large part of his childhood near the sea at Veracruz. While still in his twenties, he was keeping company with many of Latin America's foremost writers. In one of his books he predicted the terrible Mexico City earthquake of 1985, twenty years before it happened. A prolific poet and one of Mexico's foremost writers, he won the National Poetry Prize for his book *No me preguntes como pasa el tiempo* (*Don't Ask Me How the Time Goes By*) in 1969.

OCTAVIO PAZ was born in a suburb of Mexico City in 1914. He fell in love with literature early through his grandfather's vast library. He is considered one of the greatest and most beloved writers of all Latin America and won the Nobel Prize for literature in 1990. Two of his many books are *A Tree Within* and *The Labyrinth of Solitude*. He has traveled widely throughout the world and was Mexico's ambassador to India from 1962 to 1968. He has described himself as "a man in love with silence who can't stop talking." He also says, "Poetry is the memory of a country, of language. Without poetry, people can't even talk well."

CARLOS PELLICER (1899–1977) was born in Villahermosa, Tabasco, a low-lying coastal state north of Chiapas containing many huge rivers. He was a university professor of modern poetry and a director of the Ministry of Fine Arts specializing in museums. He received the National Literature Prize in 1964. His poetry is said to emphasize "music and color."

MANUEL PONCE was born in Michoacán in 1913 and recently died. He and his two brothers were orphaned at an early age. At thirteen he entered the seminary at Morelia and was ordained to the priesthood in 1936. He also worked as a seminary professor of literature for many years. He loved study, prayer, books, and abstract formulas. He founded various religious and cultural organizations in Mexico and was known as a mystical poet. He also founded a journal called *Trento* and published many collections of poems including *El Jardín Increíble* (*The Incredible Garden*). The Universidad Autónoma in Mexico City has published his *Complete Poems*.

ERIKA RAMÍREZ DIEZ was born in Celaya, Guanajuato, in 1962. She is licensed in psychology and also has many years of experience working with children in poetry workshops ("Taller de poesia infantil"). Her collections of poems include *Como digo silencio* in 1992. She now lives in Zapopan, Jalisco.

MARIO RANGEL was born in Mexico City in 1938. He studied at the Professional Studio for Engraving at Las Esmeralda. His engravings have appeared in exhibitions in various cities in the United States and Mexico.

ALFONSO REYES (1889–1959) was a teacher and a diplomat. He published over 100 books of prose and poetry and edited anthologies.

GILDA RINCÓN has published her poems for children in *Costal de Versos y Cuentos* from CONAFE (Consejo Nacional de Fomento Educativo) in Mexico City. She also composed the verses for a collection of children's songs entitled *The Sower.*

MARGARITA ROBLEDA MOGUEL was born in Mérida in 1950. She studied for the theater and has written more than twenty books for children. A musician, storyteller, singer, and comedian, she has represented the Mexican government on international cultural tours. One of her books is called *What You Can Do, You Can Do.* She lives in Mexico City.

JAIME SABINES was born in 1925 in Tuxtla Gutiérrez, Chiapas. He studied in Mexico City and has earned his living as a businessman in Chiapas. He has also published many books of poems. One series of poems was written in the voice of a father to his son.

JESÚS CARLOS SOTO MORFÍN, son of Guadalupe Morfín, was born in 1984 and wrote the poems included here when he was eight years old. He loves to play football and attends the Instituto de Ciencias primary school at the Jesuit Fathers' College in Guadalajara. His younger brother, Daniel, also writes and publishes poetry.

GERARDO SUZAN was born in Mexico City in 1963. He received his diploma in graphic design from the National School of Plastic Arts. He has illustrated many books for children in Mexico and the United States and has won various prizes for his illustrations in Mexico, Japan, and the United States.

JOSÉ JUAN TABLADA (1871–1945) was considered by many to be the first modern Mexican poet. He visited Japan in 1900 and is especially well-known for having introduced haiku, an ancient Japanese style of poetry, into the Spanish language. An art critic and journalist, he was an outspoken champion of modern painting, both Mexican and foreign. His work is still widely published throughout Mexico.

LETICIA TARRAGÓ was born in Veracruz in 1940. In 1962, she won the first prize at the Salon de la Plástica Mexicana for her engraving *Romance of the Moon.* She has designed the scenery for many plays, including the children's drama *Did Anyone Say Dragon?* An avid traveler, she has lived and worked in Poland and New Orleans, pursuing new techniques and ideas. She has also investigated painting techniques for ceramics and glazed tiles.

ROMIN TERATOL is from Zinacantan, a small Mayan community in the highlands of Chiapas. As a boy he spent many days in the woods with his slingshot. When he went to school, his shoulder-length hair was cut off. Without any brothers, he says, he never learned to fight. Once he won 160 marbles in a game with his friends. Later he became a puppeteer and served as typist, transcriber, and translator of hundreds of native texts for the Harvard Chiapas Project. He has five children and is famous for his stories and jokes.

MANUEL ULACIA was born in 1954 and studied architecture and literature. He has been a professor at the Universidad Autónoma in Mexico City and at Yale University and has published poems as well as a study of Luis Cernuda. In his poem "The Stone at the Bottom," he remembers "talking with other children in the cool shade of tall trees" and says, "Tomorrow, tomorrow, always tomorrow/and the house grows larger,/while my mother's hair turns gray/. . . and my grandmother becomes a child again./Tomorrow, tomorrow, always tomorrow" (translated by Reginald Gibbons).

QUETZALCOATL VIZUEL writes contemporary stories for children using traditional Mexican motifs. "The Pilgrim Dogs" previously appeared in *Mi Libro de Navidad: Cuentos, Canciones, y Pasatiempos* published in Mexico City by SITESA in 1987.

TERESA ZIMBRÓN's small, highly detailed work suggests personal voyages—often involving maps, Mexican iconography, or a concern for women's issues. She lives with her husband, the artist Alberto Castro Leñero, in Mexico City.

A NOTE ON THE FOLKTALES

On *The Three Suns* and *The Toad and a Buzzard*:
For Zinacantec Indians, little distinction is made between myths, fairy tales, legends, and personal histories. Dreams carry weight similar to the weight of "true" daily life. It is said that "all stories are simply 'talk' in which fantasies are as believable as actual events." Zinacantecs view their own community as the center of the world, even though many of their tales appear in other forms elsewhere in Mexico. Rodents appear frequently in North American tales, but the specific elements in *The Three Suns* are particular to the Mayan area. Romin Teratol's tale "expresses the central tenet of Zinacantec moral philosophy that food must be

shared equally. Because of their stinginess, the older brothers become food for their younger brother . . . . The tortillas that Xut stuck on his brothers' faces to turn them into pigs are a small oval variety with a hole in the center. In everyday life they are given to little children to induce them to learn to talk, on the theory that the hole in the center inspires them to open their mouths." (*The People of the Bat*, collected and translated by Robert M. Laughlin, Smithsonian Institution Press, Washington, D.C., 1988).

Buzzards and buzzard men appear in many New World stories. One common characteristic of these creatures is their foul odor which is, of course, simply connected to their fondness for eating carrion.

On *Fire and the Opossum*:
This is a popular legend in Mexico, particularly among the Indians around Oaxaca. The story we include here is a verbatim transcript of a tale as told by a Mazateco elder to an interviewer.

On *The Rabbit's Ears*:
Stories about "Rabbit" are popular not only in Mexico but throughout the New World. Rabbit is a clever, mischievous, and happy character who likes to trick the other animals. Although he is a rascal, Rabbit is generally the hero of these stories. This legend is from the Maya people of southern Mexico.

On *The Pilgrim Dogs*:
This is an original story, not a folktale, but Mexican writers often draw from their historical past, using shared cultural elements and motifs. The significance of the dog character dates to ancient times, when dogs were often buried with people who died in order to guide them through the underworld to Mictlan, the sacred place reserved for the dead. What is also wonderful about this story is the inclusion of the ancient Náhuatl language of Mexico and Central America.

A NOTE ON THE TRANSLATIONS AND TRANSLATORS

The translators for selections in *The Tree Is Older Than You Are* are, as always in bilingual texts, the quiet heroes of this volume. Some of them, such as Eliot Weinberger of New York City, have long, distinguished careers in the field. Some (Judith Infante and Joan Darby Norris, for example) were born in the United States but have lived extensively in Mexico. Others (Yvette Grutter) migrated in the other direction. Robert M. Laughlin has worked in linguistic research with the Tzotzil-speaking Maya of Chiapas since 1960. Some (W. S. Merwin, Denise Levertov, Muriel Rukeyser) are beloved, widely known poets themselves. Others (C. M. Mayo, Consuelo de Aerenlund, Raúl Aceves, to name a few) are citizens or residents of Mexico engaged in the active literary networks of their regions. We are grateful to all of them for their diligent, dedicated labors.

The poems and stories collected in this book were originally written in Spanish unless otherwise noted.

ACKNOWLEDGMENTS

The scope of this volume made it occasionally difficult—despite sincere and sustained effort—to locate poets and/or their executors. The compiler and editor regret any omissions or errors. If you wish to contact the publisher, corrections will be made in subsequent printings.

Raúl Aceves, for "Birds" by Ramiro Lomelí, translated by Raúl Aceves with Alejandro Vargas, translation copyright © by Raúl Aceves; and for "Homenaje a las islas galletas," "Homenaje a una niña en su columpio," and "Homenaje a un jardín de hipocampos," copyright © Raúl Aceves.

Homero Aridjis, for "A la orilla del agua," "El cacto," "El día que dejó," "Momento," "Noche en la cocina," "Patos," and "Si el gorrión perdiera sus alas," copyright © 1994 Homero Aridjis, from *Antología poética*, published by Fondo de Cultura Económica, Mexico.

Arte de Oaxaca and Nancy Mayagoitia, for assistance in obtaining permissions for *Fotografía* by Enrique Flores, *Angel azul* and *Serenata mexicana* by Rodolfo Morales, and *Una tarde en Juchitán* by Fernando Olivera.

Arte Nucleo Galeria and Diana Ripstein de Nankin, for providing the image for *Canto de coyotes* by Julia López and for assistance in obtaining permission.

Raúl Bañuelos, for "Agua y tierra" and "Y el niño un barco," copyright © 1994 by Raúl Bañuelos, from *Casa de sí,* published by Universidad Autónoma in Mexico City.

Alberto Blanco, for "Barcos," "Canción de enero," "Canción de mayo," and "Pasajera," copyright © Alberto Blanco, and for "También los insectos son perfectos," copyright © Alberto Blanco and CIDCLI, S.C.: all rights reserved.

Carrington/Gallagher, Ltd. and Alice Carrington and Patricia Gallagher, for providing the image for *Cruzando la línea* by Teresa Zimbrón and for assistance in obtaining permission.

Centro de Información y Desarrollo de la Comunicación y la Literatura Infantiles (CIDCLI), for "Lavanderas del Grijalva" by Rosario Castellanos, "Derecho de propiedad" and "Sobresalto" by Elías Nandino, "Mundo escondido" by José Emilio Pacheco, "La oración en el huerto" by Manuel Ponce, "Sol de Monterrey" by Alfonso Reyes, and "La tortuga" by José Juan Tablada, copyright © 1983 by CIDCLI, S.C.: all rights reserved, from *La Luciérnaga: Antología para niños de la poesía mexicana contemporánea,* compiled by Francisco Serran, published by CIDCLI, S.C., Mexico; for "de Coleadas" by Luis Miguel Aguilar, copyright © 1991 by Luis Miguel Aguilar and CIDCLI, S.C.: all rights reserved; for "También los insectos son perfectos" by Alberto Blanco, copyright © 1993 by Alberto Blanco and CIDCLI, S.C.: all rights reserved; for "La plaza" by Antonio Deltoro, copyright © 1990 by Antonio Deltoro and CIDCLI, S.C.: all rights reserved; for "Despertar," "Embrujo," "Marinero," "Nieve," and "Suéter" by Alberto

at the Grijalva" by Rosario Castellanos; "Belly Button," "Enchantment," "Sailor," "Snow Cone," "Sweater," and "Waking" by Alberto Forcada; "Lullaby" by Leticia Herrera Alvarez; "The Swallow" by Eduardo Martínez; "Andrea" and "Mothers with a Baby" by Guadalupe Morfín; "Natalia's Questions" by Myriam Moscona; "Property Rights" by Elías Nandino; "The Poet Pencil" and "The Moon, a Banana" by Jesús Carlos Soto Morfín; and "The Turtle" by José Juan Tablada, translated by Judith Infante, translations copyright © Judith Infante; for "The Apple" by José Gorostiza, translated by Judith Infante and Joan Darby Norris, translation copyright © Judith Infante and Joan Darby Norris; and for permissions-related translation assistance during the production of this book.

Christopher Johnson, for "*from* Homage to the Cookie Islands" by Raúl Aceves, translated by Christopher Johnson, translation copyright © Christopher Johnson.

Martha Black Jordan, for "Ducks" and "Should the Sparrow Lose Its Wings" by Homero Aridjis, translation copyright © Martha Black Jordan; and for "La nieta gitana" and "The Gypsy Granddaughter," original and translation copyright © Martha Black Jordan.

Robert M. Laughlin, for "I Am a Peach Tree" by Pancho Ernantes Ernantes, "The Toad and a Buzzard" by Reymunto Komes Ernantes, and "The Three Suns" by Romin Teratol, translated by Robert M. Laughlin, translations copyright © Robert M. Laughlin.

Ramiro Lomelí, for "*de* Versos de la ciudad" and "Los pájaros," copyright © Ramiro Lomelí.

Julia López, for *Canto de coyotes,* copyright © 1992 by Julia López, property of Arte Nucleo Galeria, S.A. de C.V.

Julio López Segura, for *Niño adorando al sol,* copyright © 1993 by Julio López Segura.

C. M. Mayo, for "The Plaza" by Antonio Deltoro, and "Balloon" and "The Fly" by Eduardo Hurtado, translations copyright © C. M. Mayo.

Dante Medina, for "*de* Carta explicándole a la niña Paola el vuelo del colibrí" and "Carta recordando el perro que tuvo Agnés," copyright © Centro de Estudios Literarios, Universidad de Guadalajara, Mexico.

Luis Medina Gutiérrez, for "Balneario," "Cautiva," "Devolver el agua," "Naranjada," and "Tritón," copyright © Luis Medina Gutiérrez.

Víctor Manuel Mendiola, for "La enredadera," copyright © Víctor Manuel Mendiola.

W. S. Merwin, for "Prayer to the Corn in the Field," and "Story of the Lazy Man and the Ants," translations copyright © W. S. Merwin.

Milagros Contemporary Art and Karen Rymer, for providing the image for *La novia* by Julio Galán and for granting permission to reprint the art.

Rodolfo Morales, for *Angel azul* and *Serenata mexicana,* copyright © Rodolfo Morales.

Guadalupe Morfín, for "Andrea," and "Las mamás con bebé," copyright © Guadalupe Morfín.

Angelina Muñiz-Huberman, for "El cabalista," and "La hechicera," copyright © Angelina Muñiz-Huberman.

New Directions Publishing Corporation, for "And So You Go, Never to Come Back" by José Emilio Pacheco, translated by George McWhirter, translation copyright © 1975, 1987 by George McWhirter, from *José Emilio Pacheco: Selected Poems*; and for translations from *Octavio Paz: Selected Poems*: "*from* Duration," translated by Denise Levertov, translation copyright © 1965 by Octavio Paz and Denise Levertov Goodman; "At the Door," "Objects," "Reliefs," and "Vision" translated by Muriel Rukeyser, copyright © 1973 by Octavio Paz and Muriel Rukeyser; and "Last Dawn," translated by Eliot Weinberger, translation copyright © 1979 by Octavio Paz and Eliot Weinberger.

Joan Darby Norris, for translations of "*from* Wags" by Luis Miguel Aguilar; "And the Child A Boat" by Raul Bañuelos; "To a Little Bird" by Celedonio Junco de la Vega; "They Lit a Campfire in the Mountains" by Francisco Gabilondo Soler; "*from* Verses of the City" by Ramiro Lomelí; "Captive," "Orangeade," "Return the Water," "The Bathing Place," and "Triton" by Luis Medina Gutiérrez; "Meteor" and "Somersault" by Elías Nandino; "Hidden World" by José Emilio Pacheco; "Brother Sun" by Carlos Pellicer; "The Prayer in the Orchard" by Manuel Ponce; "I Will Never Be Able to Know the Sea" by Erika Ramírez Diez; "The Cry" by Alfonso Reyes; and "The Pilgrim Dogs" by Quetzalcoatl Vizuel, translations copyright © Joan Darby Norris; for "Homage to a Girl in a Swing" by Raúl Aceves, translated by Joan Darby Norris and Yvette Grutter, translation copyright © by Joan Darby Norris and Yvette Grutter; "Water and Earth" by Raul Bañuelos, translated by Joan Darby Norris and Yvette Grutter, translation copyright © Joan Darby Norris and Yvette Grutter; "The Apple" by José Gorostiza, translated by Joan Darby Norris and Judith Infante, translation copyright © Joan Darby Norris and Judith Infante; "Letter Remembering the Dog that Agnes Once Had" and "*from* Letter Explaining the Hummingbird's Flight to Little Paola" by Dante Medina, translated by Joan Darby Norris and Barry Norris, translation copyright © Joan Darby Norris and Barry Norris; "The Woodpecker" by Gilda Rincón, translated by Joan Darby Norris and Chan Kin Norris, translation copyright © by Joan Darby Norris and Chan Kin Norris; and for "There Once Was a Girl" and "The Moon is Yours" by Jaime Sabines, translated by Joan Darby Norris and Barry Norris, translation copyright © Joan Darby Norris and Barry Norris.

Chan Kin Norris, for *Moon and Sun Together,* copyright © 1988 by Chan Kin Norris; and for "The Woodpecker" by Gilda Rincón,

INDEX OF WRITERS AND ARTISTS

LIST OF ILLUSTRATIONS